BORROWED TIME

Diane Benefiel

PRAISE FOR USA TODAY BESTSELLING AUTHOR DIANE BENEFIEL

Solitary Man

NATIONAL READERS' CHOICE AWARD WINNER

"I am in love with this story. I devoured this book and didn't want it to end. The chemistry between the characters and the plot kept me wanting to read late into the night. This is my first read from Diane Benefiel but definitely not my last. I can't wait to read more from this amazing author. Thank you Diane Benefiel for getting me hooked on your books!" ~ CJ's Book Corner

"Ryder was exactly who Brenna needed in her life, and trust me when I say you will love him because yeah he really is that good of a guy. Solitary Man is my first book by this author and it will not be the last. I really think you all will enjoy this one as much as I did it is one I do recommend." ~ I'm A Sweet And Sassy Book Whore

"I really enjoyed this book and there were a few twists and turns that kept me completely involved in the story. This is the first time I have read this author and it definitely won't be my last!" ~ Sassy Southern Book Blog

THE JAMESONS U.S. MARSHALS SERIES

Hidden Betrayal

"As someone who never pre-orders ANYTHING, I put my order in a WEEK before it came out. Know why? Because I just didn't want to wait! Not to give away any spoilers but this is my favorite book from this author yet, in no small part because Mikayla is my favorite type of heroine. Right from the get-go, she's absolutely determined to meet everything on her terms. I loved the dialogue between her and Linc--with her saying, "I didn't stay back because *I* was handling it." Yes, he's a hottie with a protective streak, but she's certainly no *little woman. It really WORKS. In the end, 10/10. Can't wait to pre-order the next one too!"* ~Amelia

"An exciting, romantic read with a sexy hero and a determined heroine who is hell-bent on doing things her own way. The romance heats up as the plot thickens. Linc and Mikayla need to work together to survive, but along the way, the sparks start flying. You need to read this!" ~danube eichinger

Hidden Judgment

"Don't buy this book if you want to get anything done!! I couldn't put it down! I laughed, I cried, I felt all the emotions that a brilliantly written romance novel brings. I am anxiously awaiting the third novel in the series!" ~Sandy Morris

"I couldn't put this book down. I thoroughly enjoyed the story line and the characters. Diane Benefeil does a great job bringing her characters to life, and weaves a compelling story. Looking forward to the next installment of this series!" ~Becca E H

HIGH SIERRAS SERIES

Flash Point

"Diane Benefiel takes us on a story filled with mystery, suspense, and action as we try to solve what is going on in the small town of Hangman's Loss. Flash Point is a story that will have you flipping the pages and wondering who is the behind the attacks against Hangman's newest resident and why." ~ Sarah Reads

*"**Flash Point** really surprised me. It's not what I was expecting but I really enjoyed reading it. It's a fun easy read that captured me from the start."* ~ Coffee Chat

Dead Giveaway

"Diane has written yet another winner in her High Sierra series. Murder witness and 'person of interest' Gwen flees with her godson to Cameron's uncle Eli. Gwen and Eli have no use for one another but come together for Cameron's sake and to find the true murderer...and in the process find their way to one another. My evening with Gwen and Eli couldn't have been more delightful, and I look forward to the next installment of the High Sierras." ~seniorphotog

"I loved this second book in the High Sierras series. This is a story of two people who are attracted to each other, but reconnecting under the worst of circumstances. I discovered Ms. Benefiel's books and have loved the careful way she draws you in to the story with characters that make you feel as if you are reading about friends. I am really looking forward to the next High Sierras book, **Already Gone.**" ~paytonpuppy

Already Gone

"This series has only gotten better and better! Seriously, there's something that really speaks to my heart about Maddy and Logan, and Hangman's Loss FEELS like a small California town tucked away in the Sierras. They're such a power couple! I read this book in just a couple of days--totally sucked me in. It's that perfect blend of fun, sizzle, and suspense! I just want to live in Maddy's life forever but since I can't--I can't wait for the next book!" ~Katharine Montgomery

"A wonderful story about second chances. The minute you start reading, you will be instantly hooked. The author weaves a tale of drama and romance that keeps you enthralled and turning the pages. Maddie is feisty and Logan is her brooding and over protective suffering hero. The sparks fly every time they see each other. Eventually they give in and realize that they are perfect for each other and have always been. This is a great story right up to the last word." ~Simatsu

Burnover in Rescued Anthology

"Sweet, Sexy stories featuring furbabies and helping to save lives, it's a win win for all." ~Kara's Books

"8 stories by 8 outstanding authors. In these stories, there is a tattoo artist, two firefighters, two sheriff deputies, a famous furniture maker, a veterinarian, and a country music singer, and I loved them all. Then add in that each story has a dog or puppy that is rescued, along with a story of love and romance, it is a winning combination." ~Susan D

Deadly Purpose

I loved everything about this book, and it made me want to check out the other books in the series! The immediate suspense drew me in, and the High Sierras setting was perfect, as was the mysterious stranger Meg finds in her cabin. This novel had a well-written, exciting, and descriptive narrative that kept me glued from start to finish. Without giving away spoilers, the author has crafted one exciting, romantic ride, full of twists and turns. I highly recommend this book and can't wait to see what the author comes up with next. ~Sebastian Moran

This book took me by surprise. I didn't expect to get so caught up in this book that my whole day was spent captured in its pages. It has been a long time since I couldn't put a book down but Deadly Purpose did this to me. I loved every page. ~WildfireJane

Clear Intent

"I'd been waiting on this one awhile!! I truly loved the story! I laughed, cried and got so frustrated I couldn't see straight! I'm now hoping there will be more from Hangman's Loss, I don't want to see this series end! Thank you for a very wonderful getaway!! I highly

recommend this complete series!!!! Wow! Just Wow!!" ~Linda Helms

"I've looked forward to every book in this series and have enjoyed each one, loving the characters as it feels you walk with them through exciting, scary situations and sigh as relationships become beautiful. This was an exciting story with almost nonstop action and heart stopping dangers. All of my favorite people in Hangman's Loss are together to help Jack, Dory, Adrian and the town through crisis." ~JLocke

Break Away

"Oh man did I love this book. It was well written and has a great storyline. It's emotional and has a nice amount of suspense. I really need to go back and read the first six books in the series. Now saying that, this book definitely reads as a standalone. I haven't read the first six books, but I never felt lost or like I am missing anything with this story. You will obviously have some small spoilers since the books are all connected. ~CrazyBookLover

"Break Away is Diane Benefiel's seventh book in the High Sierra series and is definitely a second chance at romance. Zoey had a high school crush on Levi, and when he returns home after many years, she realises her feelings have not diminished. I'm a sucker for the sexy, broody bad boy vibe, and Levi has it in spades! But the storyline also has emotion, danger and a powerful attraction that is not only undeniable, but totally unavoidable too. These characters have great chemistry and the romantic suspense plot is well written and a real page-turner." ~Arch_Angel

www.BOROUGHSPUBLISHINGGROUP.com

PUBLISHER'S NOTE: This is a work of fiction. Names, characters, places and incidents either are the product of the author's imagination or are used fictitiously. Any resemblance to actual events, locales, business establishments or persons, living or dead, is coincidental. Boroughs Publishing Group does not have any control over and does not assume responsibility for author or third-party websites, blogs or critiques or their content.

BORROWED TIME
Copyright © 2020 Diane Benefiel

All rights reserved. Unless specifically noted, no part of this publication may be reproduced, scanned, stored in a retrieval system or transmitted in any form or by any means, electronic, mechanical, photocopying, recording, or otherwise, known or hereinafter invented, without the express written permission of Boroughs Publishing Group. The scanning, uploading and distribution of this book via the Internet or by any other means without the permission of Boroughs Publishing Group is illegal and punishable by law. Participation in the piracy of copyrighted materials violates the author's rights.

ISBN 978-1-953810-11-3

To Kevin, my own personal hero.

*And to my children, Katharine and Ethan.
It is a wonderful feeling when your children
grow up to be truly amazing adults.
I love you both.*

BORROWED TIME

Chapter One

Jon glanced around and saw a neat and tidy neighborhood slowly gentrifying. He eyed the Craftsman bungalow as he approached. Bare wood showed where window trim and sections of the porch had been stripped. Maybe she did the work herself—a heck of a job for anyone. A pole sander and can of wood putty sat near the screen door, the front door open behind it. He pressed the bell and heard the scrambling sound of nails on wood and took a hasty step back when a monster dog launched itself against the screen door, barking furiously.

A voice from inside shouted, "Down, Cooper. Sit."

The dog sat, quivering with excitement. Jon decided not to risk it lunging through the screen and going for his throat, so he stayed a few feet back. From inside the woman's voice spoke again, "There's someone at my door, Lily. Yes, yes. I'll cover your shift. Uh huh. No problem. Bye."

She approached the screen cautiously. "May I help you?"

"Jon Davidson, ma'am. I spoke to a Rane Smith about an apartment for rent."

She opened the door and stepped out. The German shepherd, purebred by the look of him, stuck his nose out from around her to sniff at his jeans. When he felt reasonably sure the dog wasn't going to go maul him, he lifted his eyes to study her. Rane Smith. This was the first time he'd seen her other than the file photos. Dark hair, longer than in the last photo they had of her, fell straight past her shoulders and framed an interesting face nearly overtaken by large sea-green eyes. Pretty, lean, athletic. She sure didn't look like the type to be running with illegal drug smugglers.

She stuck a cell phone in her back pocket and held out her hand. "I'm Rane Smith."

He shook, smiled, played the part. "This is a nice neighborhood. I like the street."

"I'll be honest with you. The neighborhood is decent, but we still live in a big city and close to downtown. There've been a few break-ins. The neighbors watch out for each other, though, and we aren't afraid to call the police." Her voice held a throaty quality that reminded him of Adele.

"That's good."

She eyed him curiously. "I like to know something about who I'm renting to, so tell me about yourself, Jon. On the phone you said you're ex-military."

He launched into his carefully constructed bio. His number one rule was to stick as close to the facts as possible to avoid screwing up. Hence Jonathan David Garretson became Jon Davidson. "Yes, ma'am. US Army. I did two tours in Afghanistan, decided that was enough. I'm in training to become a firefighter."

She leaned back against the porch rail, reaching down to tug on the dog's ears. "Do you have family in Seattle?"

He stooped and held out a hand for the dog to sniff, making sure his actions were non-threatening. "No. My family is in California."

"You didn't want to live near your family? Why Seattle?"

Jon rubbed the dog's head and straightened. She was asking a lot of questions, but in her position he'd do the same. "I grew up here. My parents moved to California to be near my sister and her family, but I wanted to come back to Seattle. I like the rain." Except for his brother still living in the city, all true enough.

She flashed a smile, revealing dimples. Pretty.

"Well, you'll get plenty of it here. I'll show you the apartment. If you're still interested after you see it we'll talk some more."

Her open expression was at odds with the image he'd formed from reading her profile. He wondered who was the true Rane Smith. The profile had been sketchy, but her relationship with a member of the DiNardos, a family of drug runners, couldn't be disputed.

At his nod Rane turned and followed the half-painted porch around the corner of the house. They went down a short set of steps and along the side of the house, past a door he guessed was to the kitchen, then up to the second floor. From the top of the stairs he could see a distant glint of the bay. It looked like part of the second story had been converted to an apartment with the outside entrance added on. She took the key out of her pocket and opened the door the dog following her in.

Undercover work didn't bother him. You lied to people, got them to trust you, and used them if you had to for the job. Where the sudden twinge of guilt came from, he didn't know. Her face had revealed warmth and humor, and made him feel like a jerk for lying to her. He shook his head and took a mental step back. Looks often disguised character. The end-game would make the lies and deception worth it.

He acted like any potential tenant even though there was no way he was letting this opportunity pass. The challenge of keeping an eye on Rane Smith had become a whole lot simpler when he'd discovered she had an apartment for rent. It put him exactly where he wanted to be—close. He went through the motions of checking out the bathroom, the bedroom, the kitchenette.

"The kitchen is small so if you're a gourmet chef you'll be disappointed."

He snorted out a laugh. "Not likely. This'll do fine." He opened the refrigerator, standard size, and examined the range, one of those combo deals with the stove and oven together. He noticed the smell of fresh paint. "You do the painting yourself?" He hoped he wouldn't have to deal with a handyman underfoot.

Dimples flashed again, giving him a little tug from somewhere in his chest. "Yeah. I do what I can myself. I think it turned out okay."

She'd picked out good colors. He liked the pale green contrasted with white crown molding and wide baseboards. "Yeah," he agreed. "Looks nice."

"If you rent the apartment you'll have access to the laundry room off my kitchen."

He closed a cupboard and angled toward her. His kept his stance open and non-threatening, hands on his hips, expression neutral. All designed to gain trust. "Did you have a chance to call the references I put on my application?"

"Yes. Your references spoke highly of you."

"Good. Then are you willing to rent to me? I like the place. I think it'll work for me."

***

In the chilly early morning, Rane watched through a side window as her new tenant unloaded his truck parked in her driveway. He'd acted quickly once she'd done the background check and approved his application. In less than a week from their first meeting he was moving in. He and a guy with a wild mane of blond hair had made numerous trips up and down the stairs taking bags, boxes and furniture to the apartment. It hadn't looked like much, but maybe being in the military he hadn't accumulated a lot. She'd intended to rent to a woman, it seemed safer, but Jon's application had revealed what any landlord would want. He was reliable, had a good credit history, excellent character references, and no criminal background. Almost too good to be true.

The men hefted barbells with some serious weights attached to them up the stairs. Hmm. Guess that explains the excellent shoulders and flat belly. Not that she'd noticed. Much. She frowned as a thought struck. Put the powerful build together with the military training and he might feel comfortable sticking his nose into things better left alone.

Wonderful. Another worry on top of the one that had been staring her in the face for the past few months. Kyle got out in five days. After Sunday she'd have to start looking over her shoulder, checking the backseat of the car before getting in it. Do that paranoid recheck to be sure she'd locked all the doors and windows in the house. Maybe he'd leave her alone.

Maybe he'd never discovered her complicity in his conviction for a crime he hadn't committed. She hadn't known he'd been set up at the time of the trial, but that didn't excuse her continued silence. On the other hand, there were all the other crimes he'd committed, some really bad, that had never been prosecuted.

She sighed. In all that time in jail, he had to've guessed her father's involvement and her collusion. Worse, Simon DiNardo, Kyle's brother, had to know.

Watching Jon and his moving buddy, each holding an end of a flatscreen TV twice the size of hers going up the stairs, distracted her for a moment.

When she and Kyle were dating, he'd said they were soulmates. She'd found out later he'd cheated on her. So not soulmates. Then the girl he'd been seeing on the side had turned up dead, overdosed on heroin he'd supplied. That had been the final straw.

Maybe in these intervening years, he'd given up on the soulmate thing. A match destined by the stars didn't lead to prison. Rane rubbed a fist against her forehead to ease the tension headache that she could feel forming there. The situation with Kyle was such a complicated mess. If he'd figured out her father had anything to do with sending him to prison for the past three years, he'd have more than an old relationship as a reason to come for her. When he was done with her, he'd go after her dad. No, she wouldn't be sleeping easy.

Moving away from Seattle and the DiNardos' sphere of influence to find someplace safer hadn't been feasible. Her father's illness had prevented that. His doctors, his friends, everything he knew was here. So instead, she'd put together what she called her "what if" scenarios.

What if Kyle broke into her house? What if he came to the hospital while she was working? What if he found her father?

With her "what ifs" in mind, she'd devised plans to keep them safe. None of which included contacting the police. That would bring the whole house of cards crashing down.

What had once been the backbone of her support system was now to be avoided at all costs. Whatever happened she had to take care of it herself. Calling the police was simply not an option.

Forcing herself to stop chewing on her bottom lip, she let Cooper into the house before gathering her backpack. She made sure the dog door was locked, and grabbed her cell and keys. Ready for her shift, she reached down and rubbed Cooper along his neck. Besides being her best buddy, her dog was another layer of protection.

"You be good, baby. Don't open the door for any bad guys."

He hung his head, then slid down to lie on the floor, nose on his paws. The pathetic look he gave her turned the guilt screws. She was sure he did it on purpose.

"I'm sorry, okay? I gotta go to work and make the money to pay for those gourmet doggie treats." Cooper refused to meet her eyes. "Great. Another guilt-trip." She wondered if she was the only person who had conversations with her dog and believed he understood every word.

She set the house alarm at the keypad on the wall, then let herself out the kitchen door to Cooper's muffled whine, locking the handset and deadbolt behind her.

Jon jogged down the stairs from his apartment. She should've kept walking but for some reason found herself waiting for him.

Everything about him was lowkey and shouldn't spark concern, but she felt there was more to him than he let on. He was overly watchful. His dark blue eyes seemed to take in every detail of his surroundings, and he had an underlying intensity that belied the laidback image he projected.

He came to a stop at the bottom of the stairs, and she wondered if their meeting was coincidental.

She studied him, trying to figure out what set her senses buzzing. A faded army t-shirt over a white thermal showed off his wide shoulders, and his jeans fit exactly how they should. Short blondish brown hair and deep blue eyes over killer cheekbones and a short scar on his chin gave her a little pull and made her wish she was what she appeared to be.

"Hey. Going to work?" He stopped at the bottom of the stairs, tucking his hands in his back pockets.

Rane looked down at her dark green scrubs. For warmth she'd added a cream-colored long-sleeved t-shirt underneath. "What gave it away?"

He smiled, showing not quite straight teeth. "The dog. Sounds like he knows you're not going to the mailbox."

Since Cooper whined again she had to nod in agreement. "Yeah. He lets me know he's not happy when I leave for work. He'll be fine in a few minutes." She backed away with a wave and started walking down the driveway. "See you."

"Wait. Isn't your car in the garage? You need a ride?"

Without turning back, she called out, "walking today" and continued to the street. Kyle's imminent release meant soon she wouldn't have the freedom of walking to work.

Eight blocks later Rane let herself in the employee entrance at the back of the hospital. She cleared the inner security door and became immersed in the sounds and smells of St. Augustine's. Her world for the next twelve hours. After dumping her things in her locker, she walked through swishing doors into the emergency room and her chaotic, crazy job as a certified emergency nurse.

An OD, a skateboarder with a broken arm, and a child with an ear infection kept her busy for the next hour. It was way longer than that before she found twenty minutes for her first break. She pumped quarters into the vending machine and listened to a can of soda clunk down, hoping it didn't wake Dr. Grayson who lay zonked out on the long vinyl sofa. He didn't seem comfortable. She leaned against a table looking out the window into the late afternoon sky and drank her dose of caffeine cold.

Lily came in through the swinging doors with food from the cafeteria in her hands. "Here's your sandwich. Better eat fast. I heard there's a multicar that includes a commuter bus on the five. We're about to get slammed."

Rane took the sandwich from her friend, examining the unappetizing blob of what the label identified as tuna salad between two slices of bread. She needed to remember to pack her lunch. "Do you think we should wake Dr. G?"

Lily looked over her shoulder at the sleeping man. Their secret was that the G wasn't for Grayson but for gorgeous. He was true eye candy. "No." Lily talked around her bite of sandwich. "They'll come looking for him soon enough. Let him sleep."

Rane knew Lily looked out for him. She'd been in lust for months, and despite Rane pushing Lily to at least *flirt* with the guy, she'd done nothing. She'd convinced herself she wasn't his type. "Sam Grayson goes for blondes," Lily had told Rane. Looking at her friend now, she knew Lily didn't recognize how well her mixed heritage worked for her. Chinese, Hispanic, and white gave Lily a beautiful skin tone of the lightest amber, exotically tilted golden brown eyes, and a fit body with curves Rane envied.

She swallowed down the last of her sandwich as the call came over the speaker. She looked at her friend. "That's us."

When she finally left the hospital, the sun lay low across Puget Sound silhouetting the rugged outline of the Olympic Peninsula. She liked walking home at the end of shift and in late September the city pulsed with people jamming in outdoor time before fall rain took over. Bicyclists pumped up the hill in their vivid jerseys while a man pushed twin girls in a baby jogger.

Walking past cafés and shops, Rane caught snatches of conversation and the flicker of candlelight. She felt herself relaxing, enjoying the cool breeze bringing the smells of the wharf. She trudged up the hill, then a few blocks north where the buildings transitioned from business to residential.

Traffic thinned and she turned onto her street. She heard the whoops and yelling of children playing on the wide lawns fronting the houses. She waved to an elderly couple holding hands sitting on a porch swing. Starting up the sidewalk to her house, she thought if she had the energy to make dinner maybe she'd take it out onto her porch and eat in a padded wicker chair.

"Hey."

Rane jumped, her heart in her throat, the can of pepper spray out of her pocket and her finger on the pump before she could form a coherent thought.

"Whoa. Steady there." The figure sitting on her top step rose to stand, hands up.

"Jon." His name escaped her in a rush. Not Kyle. Jon. Kyle was still in prison.

"Yeah. Do you mind taking your finger off the trigger? I was sprayed with that stuff in the army. I could do without it tonight."

"Okay." Breathing deep to settle her racing heart, she lowered the can. "What are you doing out here? You startled me."

"Sorry. Been enjoying the evening." He cocked his head. "You okay?"

She nodded. "Sorry about that. I carry the pepper spray because, hey, I live in a big city. I haven't had to use it yet."

His smile remained easy, and Rane had the distinct impression he was being careful so she wouldn't threaten to blind him again.

"Can I get you a beer?" he asked.

She considered the offer. She didn't get any weird vibes from him. Only *I'm a nice guy so don't pepper spray me* kind of vibes. "Okay. A beer sounds good."

"Great. Back in a second."

He jogged around the corner of the house and she heard him pounding up the stairs. A whine sounded from inside the house. She unlocked her door and stepped in to greet a joyous Cooper. She deactivated the house alarm, leaving the screen latched and the door open to let in the evening breeze.

She dumped her backpack and keys on a bench and took the dog into the backyard. She was being stupid. Feeling attracted to Jon was exactly why she shouldn't sit outside having a beer with him. She didn't do relationships, especially with her dangerous ex about to get out of prison.

But Jon didn't seem interested in her that way. They were having a low risk beer. Besides, she could hardly back out now without the situation getting awkward. She stepped back onto the porch as he returned, holding two open bottles by their long necks.

Taking one, she sat beside him on the second step. She tried not to think about Kyle getting out in a few days. She needed to be normal. Just hanging out with her renter. She searched for something to talk about. "This must be quite a change from Afghanistan."

He gave a short laugh, then took a sip of his beer. "You can't even imagine. Over there I would have sold a kidney for a cold brew at the end of the day."

"What did you do there? What kind of work?" She wasn't simply making conversation, she wanted to know.

He shrugged. "When I first started out, it was a lot of patrols. We'd flush out the Taliban, avoid IEDs. Avoid getting dead. This last tour it was entirely training Afghan soldiers."

"Did you enjoy it?"

He set down his bottle and leaned back, elbows supporting him on the top step. "Enjoy it? Most people ask if I hated it."

Rane studied him in the fading light. He seemed focused on the street, gaze intent. "Well, did you?"

"I liked some things about the country. It's beautiful. Wild. The people are amazingly resilient and hard working. But I hated always feeling on edge, like my world could blow up, literally, at any given moment."

Rane thought about that as she looked out into the evening.

"What about you? You work at a hospital?"

"Yeah. I'm an ER nurse at St. Augustine's." She thought about getting up and turning on the porch light, but decided it was nice in the deep twilight.

"You must see a lot of horrible things."

"I do," she agreed. "But I know I'm doing something good."

"That's important."

They sat quietly for a couple of minutes. She found she enjoyed talking to him and felt a little hum of pleasure at being able to relax.

"Is your family here in Seattle?"

"Yeah." She didn't like talking about her family. People always asked about her mother.

He gave a short laugh. "C'mon, Rane. This is how conversations work. I share a little, you share a little. Then maybe we get to know each other a bit." He sat forward resting his forearms on his knees, head cocked at her.

She shrugged before responding. "I don't have much family to talk about. It's me and my dad. That's it."

"Your mom?"

"Took off when I was a kid. Made a new life for herself somewhere that's not here."

"Ah. So what does your dad do?"

"Dad was a cop. He's retired now." She wondered if she imagined a heightened interest.

"A beat cop? A detective?"

"Detective. You can't really want to know about my dad. What made you decide to join the military?

He sipped his beer, and she wondered if she was imagining there was something more than friendship behind the conversation. "Nope. Still your turn. Tell me about your day at St. Augustine's. I bet in some ways it resembles a typical day in Afghanistan."

Rane saw his gaze drift to her mouth. She tried to keep her train of thought. "It sounds like what's similar is that there is no typical day."

He nodded. "So tell me."

She stretched her legs out in front of her. "Well, today started off with an OD. Heroin. Parents are getting ready for work this morning and their seventeen-year-old boy doesn't wake up to catch the school bus."

"Did he make it?"

She shot him a questioning look at the urgency in his voice.

"Yeah. But surviving today is only the first step. The kid has a lot to go through before he's okay."

He nodded. His tone was even when he spoke. "I wonder how a seventeen-year-old hooks up with heroin."

She lifted a shoulder. "They don't start with heroin. He probably pill-partied or found some Oxy in his parents' medicine cabinet. Got hooked and took the step to heroin. It's cheaper and easier to obtain." Rane stifled a yawn at the same time the dog whined at the door. She drained the last of her beer. "It's time to feed Cooper. Thanks for the beer and the conversation."

Jon rose to his feet and put a hand down for her, palm up. She hesitated before laying her hand in his, their gazes met as he pulled her to her feet. He held her hand a moment longer than necessary before releasing her. "You're welcome."

In the glow of the streetlight she gave him a quick nod and retreated into the house.

Chapter Two

Rane turned off her bedside lamp and burrowed under the covers. A warm shower, a little TV and thirty minutes reading should've calmed her mind, but she still felt edgy. Kyle's release yesterday had made her hyperalert and she'd spent the past thirty-six hours waiting for him to do something stupid, or worse. If she was lucky, he'd forgotten about her and moved on. The letters had stopped coming after his first year in prison. She'd never responded to any of them. Perhaps he'd accepted she wanted nothing more to do with him.

Or he could've figured out where the heroin under the back seat of his car had come from and was biding his time. She worried he'd come after her dad and her for revenge.

She flopped onto her back, pushing back the blanket. She'd have to quit obsessing or she would never get to sleep.

Think of something else.

Like why was it she hadn't had a date in more than three months. It wasn't from lack of male attention. When she did go out with guys, by the third or fourth date she'd start backing off. She would delay returning phone calls and texts, postpone dates, or end the evening early.

Sometimes she actually skipped the avoidance and told the guy that she didn't want to see him anymore. She didn't need an analyst to tell her she dumped before getting dumped, which had to come from her mom up and leaving when she was a kid. Rane couldn't trust someone to be there in the long run. When it came to guys, she left before they could leave her.

Great, maybe she needed therapy.

She rubbed her temple where a dull ache told her she should get up and take a couple Tylenol. But moving around would only make her more alert and less likely to fall asleep. Her mind wandered to Jon. She knew she'd been thinking about relationships because he stirred something in her that refused to settle.

She glanced at the clock on her nightstand. A minute past midnight. Thank God she didn't have to work in the morning. She closed her eyes and ordered herself to sleep. She started to drift, her breath deepening, then a noise, vague and indistinct, made her eyes fly open.

A creaking sound, then a thud outside, maybe near the kitchen. The doggy door to the backyard was locked but it sounded like someone was trying to get in that way.

In the dim glow from the flameless candles she used as nightlights she could see Cooper, head raised, ears perked. She sat up, mind racing. She wouldn't panic, she had her "what if" plans. Calm and rational, she'd protect herself.

Rational meant it didn't have to be Kyle. It could a transient forcing open the alley gate to look for bottles in the recycling bin, then wandering down her driveway. She'd even had a raccoon get stuck in her trash can once.

Her only certainty was she couldn't call the cops. If it was Kyle, the police finding him at her house would cause unwanted questions. Questions that could lead back to her father.

A growl rumbled low in Cooper's throat.

"Quiet, Cooper."

Rane slipped out of bed, heart beating double time. She had to see who was out there. Knowing if it was Kyle was better than worrying about it. Moving quietly to her closet, she opened the gun lock box with the keyed in code. Taking a steadying breath, she pulled out the Colt .45. It might be a raccoon, but it might not.

No way was she taking a chance if Kyle DiNardo was back.

With the memory of practice sessions with her father echoing in her head, she loaded the clip, pulled back the slide, and set the safety. She put a calming hand on Cooper who had moved to stand at alert next to her.

Moonlight filtered in from the skylight over the landing casting a dim glow as Rane and the dog moved to the stairs. Maybe Jon was taking out his trash. She could yell at him for scaring her, which would help release the tension cramping her neck.

Creeping through the house, gun angled down, she paused at the bottom of the stairs. Through the side window she saw a shadowy figure running up the driveway toward the garage. She dashed to the kitchen door, peering through the window into the night. The motion light at the corner of the house blazed brightly, as did the one on the far side of the garage where she kept her trashcans. A movement, a shape darker than the rest, caught her attention.

Her tenant wasn't taking out his trash. Jon was moving with stealthy purpose. He kept to the shadows. His attention focused on the side of the garage she couldn't see. His truck parked in the driveway provided cover, and he edged closer.

Rane heard a muffled thud. He must've heard it too because he raced toward the garage. He stopped and put his back against the wall, then he took a quick peek around the corner before disappearing into the dark.

She waited several long moments, mind spinning. If it was Kyle, she could deal with him better than Jon. He could be heading into danger and might need her help. He certainly moved like he could take care of himself, though. Straining, she couldn't hear anything but her own heart pounding, until another crash sounded, echoing through the windows.

She shoved the .45 into a kitchen drawer. She wouldn't confront the intruder, but she wasn't leaving Jon out there to bleed to death if he'd been attacked. Punching in the disarm code on the alarm pad, she pulled open the kitchen door. Hesitating only briefly, she slipped out, leaving a whining Cooper inside.

The cold night air made her wish she'd pulled on a sweatshirt over the tank she slept in. She hoped she hadn't made a mistake leaving the gun in the house.

She crouched in the shadow of Jon's truck. The night was alive with sound. Crickets chirped, and cars on the avenue a couple blocks over made a quiet whooshing sound. In the distance an ambulance siren wailed, likely on its way to St. Augie's. Cautiously, she rounded the truck, stopping when the backyard gate swung open to crash against the fence.

Cooper barked furiously. A blurred form streaked down the driveway, barreling into her, knocking her to her knees before racing away.

Seconds later Jon sprinted through the gate, coming to a swift stop when he saw her. "You okay?"

"Got knocked down. I'm fine."

Up the street a car engine turned over with a roar. Jon ran to the end of the driveway and she saw the glint of metal from a gun tucked into the waistband in the back of his jeans. Tires squealed as a vehicle sped away.

Rising slowly to her feet, she brushed grit from her palms. The guy who had knocked her down was dressed in dark pants and a sweatshirt with the hood up. He could've been anybody.

Wincing at pain from her knee, she held onto the side of the truck as Jon trotted up the driveway.

Voice rough, he asked, "You really okay?"

"A little bruised. Could you tell what the guy looked like?" She wasn't sure if it was from cold air or adrenaline, but she had to clench her jaw to suppress a shiver.

He shook his head. "Dark clothing, hood. Couldn't see his face, so no. He took off in a black Ford SUV. I couldn't make out the plates." He cast a frustrated glance toward the street.

"You want to go chase after him or something?"

He seemed to have to force himself to relax. "Too late for that. I don't like the idea of someone prowling around your house. You could be in danger. Anyone bothering you lately?" He offered a hand.

She took it, strong fingers helping to steady her as gingerly she put weight on her knee. "No."

"Had any bad break ups? Anyone vowing everlasting love?"

She glanced up at him, suddenly suspicious. "None." There was no way he could know about Kyle. Taking a hobbling step, she sucked in a breath. "Wow. That hurts."

"Okay, up you go."

Rane let out a squeak when he bent and scooped her into his arms. "Put me down," she ordered.

"Nope. You're hurt. I'll patch you up. Let's get you inside before you freeze."

"I'm fine. My knee's scraped, that's all."

He ignored her, carrying her toward the house. Cooper let out a bark when Jon elbowed open the door. "Get the light."

She leaned down and flipped the switch as they entered the kitchen and Jon kicked the door shut before crossing the floor to set her on the counter. He put a hand on her shoulder. "Stay put."

With the kitchen light glowing warm against dark windows, he gently rolled up her flannel pant leg to where it was torn at the knee.

Rane studied his bent head, thick hair mussed like he'd been in bed, as he bent to the task.

There was something different about him, something she couldn't put her finger on. He pulled the fabric away where blood oozed from the scraped knee. "Where are your first aid supplies?"

Before she could shove off the counter to get them Jon raised his gaze to lock on hers. "I said stay put." The difference hit her. The laidback dude was gone and the new Jon revealed a scarcely contained intensity. It was like watching layers of his personality being revealed.

"You sure are bossy all of a sudden."

When he spoke, his voice was edged with impatience. "Tell me where the bandages are."

Barely keeping herself from rolling her eyes, she motioned to a door on the far side of the kitchen. "In the bathroom off the laundry room. Bottom drawer of the vanity."

He returned a minute later, hands full of small packages. He took a moment to wash his hands and then ripped open a bag of cotton pads.

"I can do this."

When he glared at her, she tried a smile. "Really. Being an ER nurse and all, I might be able to manage it."

"I know what to do," he muttered. He cleaned the wound competently and applied antiseptic. After pressing on a bandage, he stood back. She scooted off the counter, stifling a groan when her leg took the weight.

"Can't you take it slow?" He took her hand to steady her.

"I'm fine. The soreness will be gone in a day or so." She frowned at him when he scowled. "What I don't get is why you're mad at me."

"I'm not mad at you."

"Really? Then what's with the attitude?"

"Maybe I don't like you getting hurt. Maybe I don't like you going out there at night when some guy is lurking around your house. You should've stayed inside and called nine-one-one."

He turned her hand over, his head tilted to examine it. He brushed his thumb across the abraded palm. His soothing touch contradicted his sharp words and made her acutely aware of them standing so close she could smell the outdoors on him. Forcing herself to focus, she told him, "You didn't stay inside and call nine-one-one."

"That's different." He raised his head, his blue eyes sharp like laser beams. He took a step back and she told herself it was a good thing because she could breathe without drawing in a lungful of air that smelled of him.

"Is it different because you have a gun tucked in the back of your jeans?"

He gave her a hard look. "Partly."

"Or is it because you think a guy can handle himself and a woman can't?"

He gave a humorless laugh. "Save it. I served with extremely capable women in Afghanistan who could take care of themselves in any kind of situation. I have no idea if you've been trained to defend yourself so I'm going on the assumption you haven't had more than the basics." He raised a brow. "Am I wrong?"

"Well, I haven't been trained to kill someone with my bare hands."

"Then you should've stayed inside and called the cops."

"I saw you running around the side of the garage. I thought the guy could attack you and leave you bleeding to death. I was going out to check on you. If you'd been hurt, then I would've called nine-one-one."

"Right. This would be before the guy attacked you, too. Jesus, Rane." He began gathering up the trash from the bandages. When Cooper whined Jon stopped, then looked at the dog. "Why didn't you bring the dog out with you? He'd scare the shit out of any suspect."

She shrugged. "I didn't want him hurt."

He stared, expression incredulous. "You have this big-ass German shepherd who'd go for the throat of anyone threatening you, and you didn't let him out to do his job because you thought he'd get hurt?"

She lifted a shoulder. "Well, yeah. If the guy had a gun, he could've shot Cooper. It's not worth it."

He turned away, spearing long fingers through his hair as if trying to ease his frustration. "You're something else, you know that? Next time call nine-one-one and let the dog out."

When she didn't say anything, he narrowed his eyes. "Rane? I want you to promise you'll call for help if anything like this happens again."

He refused to look away and finally she shrugged. "Okay. Fine. I'll call for help the next time I see someone lurking outside my house. Satisfied?"

He gave her a dark look. "Not nearly." He seemed to make an effort to shake off his mood. "Here's what we're going to do. I'll have another look around, make sure the gates are locked. Cooper can come with me so he can see if anything's up. You check the doors and windows around the house. I'll come back with the all-clear, then you can set the alarm. Okay?"

Ten minutes later he was back, rapping lightly on the kitchen door. When she opened it he handed her Cooper's leash. "Everything's secure. Looks like the guy tried your front windows looking for one that was open. He's long gone now."

She nodded solemnly. "Thank you."

He looked at her suspiciously. "You being sarcastic?"

"No, I'm serious. Thank you for going out there in the first place. For bandaging my knee." She shrugged. "For making me feel safe."

He whistled out a breath. "Be careful saying things like that. Men are suckers for women in need of protection."

She smiled at him. "Okay. And Jon? You should switch from firefighter training to the police academy. You're a natural."

With that, she closed the door and turned the lock.

***

Rane stood on the tall ladder with an open can of wood putty on the tray. She'd had the paint on the porch and wood trim professionally removed to deal with the lead issue, but she'd save money prepping and painting the raw wood herself.

She scooped more putty onto her knife and pressed it into a nail hole in the second-story windowsill. The day had grown warm, and sweat trickled down the small of her back under her sleeveless t-shirt. She tipped up her ball cap anchored by her ponytail, working the putty knife to fill in the imperfections.

The compound dried quickly and would soon be ready for sanding. She needed this kind of work. The incident the night before had rattled her, and not only because someone had been trying to get into her house. Her response to Jon had caught her off guard.

Being around him was like the anticipation when rollercoaster cars were being pulled up the incline, when you knew that in a moment you'd start hurtling down in a near freefall.

She shook her head as she scooped out more putty. Giving into that kind of excitement was dangerous. In addition to those mixed-up feelings, she'd visited her father that morning. That had been a good reminder that she wasn't free to pursue any kind of relationship.

At sixty-five, her dad should've been enjoying his retirement, going deep-sea fishing, and having coffee with his buddies. Instead, he spent his days watching reruns of '80s TV shows and talking to himself.

After receiving a diagnosis of early-onset Alzheimer's, he'd lived with her, and had in-home care while she was at work. For a time, she'd been able to take care of him. Gradually his condition had worsened, and she'd made the heart-wrenching decision two months ago to place him in a facility.

Though rationally she knew it was the right thing to do, and that he was safer there, she still felt tremendous guilt.

She visited him on the days she wasn't working. Most days were good, he remembered she was his daughter, and his irritability stayed in check. But today hadn't been one of those days.

She'd arrived with birdseed to fill the feeder outside his window, and he'd complained that the birds had kept him up all night. Pointing out that the birds weren't out at night would have gotten her nowhere. Instead, she had stowed the birdseed and sat with him, playing the music that sometimes soothed him.

What bothered her most was he'd brought up the DiNardo case. Today wasn't the first time. While he often forgot things she'd told him five minutes earlier, he remembered with crisp detail how he'd planted the heroin that had gotten Kyle sentenced to prison.

Back then, her dad had already started displaying subtle symptoms of the disease that would ravage his brain, making her question if the disease had contributed to his poor judgment when it came to Kyle. She wondered if her dad said anything about the case around the staff, or if they'd do anything about it if he had.

She hoped they'd think it was the ramblings of a shattered mind. What he'd done must be weighing on his conscience, causing him to want to get it out.

Holding onto the windowsill, she carefully climbed one more step on the ladder. She tapped the putty lid closed and picked up the sanding block.

"Hey, what are you doing up there?"

She looked down at Jon's upturned face. Gorgeous blue eyes and dark blond stubble along a strong jaw did nothing for her equilibrium. The little scar on his chin added to his appeal.

Images of the night before flashed through her mind. She wondered if he felt the change in their relationship. More likely, it was all in her head and there was nothing to feel.

"Rane."

God, she was losing it. "I'm running a marathon?"

"Cute." He studied her for a moment. "Would it be wrong to say I don't like you up there?"

"Yep."

"Okay, then I won't say it. Come down."

She continued using the sanding block, smoothing the dried putty until it blended into the wood. "No."

"Can I do that for you?"

"No."

"You pissed at me?"

She looked down at him again. "No."

There was no way to tell him that by renting him the apartment Kyle DiNardo might be a real danger for him. She couldn't help feeling safer knowing he'd protect her, but she couldn't shake the feeling he'd get hurt.

"You going to use wood preservative on that?" When she nodded he asked, "Where is it?"

She raised a brow at the question before answering. "There's a can in the garage."

He started toward the garage and she called after him. "You don't have to do that. Go lift weights or something."

He walked off shaking his head and she wondered why he was bothering to help her. He returned minutes later with her other ladder and the can of wood preservative.

After leaning the ladder against the wall on the opposite side of the window, he pried the lid off the can and dipped in a clean brush. "What color are you painting the trim?"

Stifling a sigh, Rane decided to answer. It seemed easier than to fight with him. "White. I'm keeping it white and the siding pine green. The front door will be a deep burgundy red."

"Nice."

She finished sanding and watched him apply the sealer with a sure hand. She fought against his pull. She didn't want to be attracted to him.

Between her father and Kyle, her life wasn't stable. With Kyle out of prison, her life could blow up at any moment. She needed calm and simple, and she had a feeling Jon would be anything but calm and simple.

Movement caught her eye, and she glanced down to the sidewalk. She bit back a groan. Mrs. Kershaw approached, decked out in a sapphire pantsuit matching the sparkling collar and leash on Honey Pumpkin, her blond Lhasa Apso.

"Yoo-hoo, Rane, sweetie. How are you?" Her neighbor sang the words.

Mrs. Kershaw, over-the-top by nature, did everything with enthusiasm, from walking the dog to growing spectacular roses. Normally, Rane enjoyed her neighbor for the simple reason that while Mrs. Kershaw might be nosy, she cared about people. She also kept an eye on the comings and goings of their neighbors, her attention to them something to do to stave off the loneliness since Mr. Kershaw died last year.

Rane often invited Mrs. Kershaw in for tea and enjoyed her company, but today's visit could be fraught with peril if she zeroed in on Jon. Not that Rane blamed her. Wearing a navy Henley and low-slung jeans, he looked good enough to eat. Not many women would be able to resist his appeal. Plus, Mrs. Kershaw loved matchmaking, and she wouldn't be subtle.

"I'm good, Mrs. Kershaw," Rane answered. "How are you and Honey Pumpkin?"

"Honey Pumpkin wanted to get out, so here we are, enjoying this beautiful sunshine."

Mrs. Kershaw's gaze fixed on the man who'd paused what he was doing to watch Honey Pumpkin waddle over to the lilac bush and lift his leg. Cooper didn't bother to get up from his shady spot on the porch. Rane thought her dog didn't consider Honey Pumpkin a canine and probably thought of him more as some sort of mobile mop.

"Is this your tenant, Rane honey?"

"This is Jon Davidson, and yes, he's renting the apartment."

Jon descended the ladder. After setting down the can of preservative, he held out his hand. "Mrs. Kershaw."

She grasped his hand in both of hers. "My, I do love a man with manners. Especially when they're handsome. You look like you're handy, too. Rane could use someone like you in her life."

"You hear that, Rane? You could use someone like me in your life." When he tilted his head up and grinned, her heart tripped. *Damn.*

She descended the ladder. "Great. Then you can finish with the preservative on that window trim while I get changed to run my errands." Errands she'd made up to avoid Jon. She gave Mrs. Kershaw a hug then set her tools on the porch.

Mrs. Kershaw cackled. "She's got your number, Jon."

"Yes, ma'am. I'd better get busy."

Rane closed the screen door behind her, wondering how she was going to keep him at arm's length when he seemed intent on closing the gap.

She had to do something to stop her reaction whenever he was near. If she didn't see him, didn't interact with him, didn't find those blue eyes watching her, then maybe this insane attraction would fizzle out.

Chapter Three

The following evening, Rane felt raw while driving home from work, her emotions exposed and bruised. Emily Johansson, a young woman who'd lived a few blocks over and had been on the brink of her adult life, was dead. A senseless, mindless death that added one more statistic in the city's growing heroin epidemic. Of all the days Rane had worked in the emergency room, this one ranked right up at the top of the worst. She let herself into the house and greeted Cooper with a rub.

Her buddy always made her feel better. She clipped on his leash. Usually, she liked walking in her neighborhood. This evening kids were outside squeezing in the last few minutes of play before being called in to do their homework.

Rick from two doors down pulled up his trashcans from the street, and Mrs. Kershaw waved at Rane as she chatted with another neighbor. Everything seemed so normal. Except this evening wasn't normal. Rane's walk took her down several blocks before she found the house she was looking for.

A group of teenagers were gathered on the front lawn. Some were in tears, others looked frightened. She talked to a couple of kids she knew before asking one of them to hold Cooper. Rane went through the open front door and found Emily's parents huddled together on the couch. She spoke a few words to them, but really, what could she say? Sorry Emily died, or any softer version of that would do nothing to alleviate their sorrow, but they listened with grief stricken faces, and thanked her.

Around the room conversations were subdued. Rane spoke with a few people until, not able to take any more, she broke away. She collected Cooper who was tolerating kids petting him and, with slumped shoulders, walked home in the deepening twilight.

Number one rule of nursing: don't get emotionally involved. A nurse couldn't survive otherwise. But every now and then feelings slipped past Rane's guard and found a way into her heart.

"Rane."

She jerked to a stop on her front lawn. Jon was sitting on her steps in the glow of the porch light, a beer in hand. So much for putting a little distance between them. "Hi."

"I didn't want to startle you, risk the pepper spray again."

She tugged her hand out of her pocket and showed him the loosely gripped can. "Good call."

She hadn't moved from the middle of the yard, but Cooper decided he wanted to visit with his new friend and tugged on the leash. Giving in, she followed the dog to the porch.

"You want to sit, relax for a few minutes?"

He must've seen the indecision on her face because he reached out a hand and tugged her down. She sat next to him and unclipped Cooper's leash so he could lie across the step at her feet.

"So?"

She turned to look at him, actually glad for the distraction. She liked the way his hair was so thick it didn't want to lie down on his forehead. "So what?"

"For a general conversation starter, you could tell me about your day."

With him gazing at her expectantly, she found herself looking away, trying to suppress the emotions simmering under the surface. "You don't want to know about my day. Tell me about yours."

"Nope. I asked first."

She remained silent several long minutes until letting out a heartfelt sigh. "My day was crappy."

He handed her his beer. "Have a sip and tell me what made it crappy."

She contemplated the bottle before taking a drink. "Two more overdoses today. One fatal." Staring out into the darkening street, what she saw was the teenage girl lying dead on a hospital bed, her parents inconsolable.

"Heroin again?"

"Yeah. Both of them." She hadn't realized her hand was still in his until he squeezed her fingers. "One girl will make it, at least for now. I hope she'll take treatment as the lifeline it is. But the other,

Emily Johansson, won't get that opportunity. I knew her. She lived only a few blocks from here." She turned to look at him, fighting the sadness. "Nineteen and her life is over because she got hooked on heroin."

He released her hand and draped an arm around her shoulder. "I'm sorry." A car drove past slowly, its headlights cutting through the dusk.

They sat for several minutes in silence, his touch comforting.

"Is that where you went on your walk?"

"Yeah. There's a lot of heartbreak out there because of some really bad drugs." She couldn't help but wonder if the DiNardo family was still behind the heroin trade in the city. It was probably a safe bet they were.

"Rane." His voice held a subdued urgency.

She looked at him. "What?"

"Do you know why someone might be watching your house?"

"Where?" She gripped the bottle tightly, glancing up and down the street.

"The gray sedan that just went past. It's parked across the street, one door down. When I turn my back to the car it'll appear you're looking at me, but I want you to look over my shoulder. He parked there earlier this afternoon, and he's there again."

Jon angled his body and, with a sinking feeling in her stomach, she looked past him to see the vehicle. There wasn't enough light to make out the driver's features but she could see his profile and she knew.

The fantasy she'd woven it hadn't been him a couple of nights ago, and that he'd leave her alone, was ludicrous. Kyle was here.

"Do you recognize the car or the driver?"

She forced her attention back to the man beside her. "Yes."

Steady blue eyes reflected the porch light. "Is he a threat?"

Rane swallowed hard. "Possibly."

He leaned forward, blocking her view. "Sweetheart, we're going to stand up and move into the house. I'll keep my arm around your shoulders so it looks like we're together."

When she tried to look past him again he leaned closer, his breath fanning her lips. He brought a hand up to touch her cheek, his gaze intent. "Don't look at him again. Follow my lead. I don't want to tip him off." He took the beer bottle she held and set it next to the post.

Standing, he pulled her up with him, keeping his arm firmly around her. Cooper scrambled to his feet to follow them.

Jon opened the screen, and when she would've flipped on the light, he tightened his grip. "Walk through to the kitchen and turn on the light in there. Put the dog in the backyard. I'll watch from here. Do something you'd normally do in the kitchen. Mess with the dishes or something like that."

Walking away from him, from the security of his nearness, was harder than she would've guessed. She fed Cooper. When he was done, she let him out and began emptying the dishwasher, her mind racing. She should get her gun. She had two. One upstairs and one down. But if she pulled out a gun Jon would certainly ask uncomfortable questions.

She'd been a fool thinking she was safe and for not taking Kyle prowling around at night as a warning. She needed to find the name of his parole officer. Most likely, Kyle would deny being here, but she'd document everything that happened nonetheless. She set plates in the cupboard and began sorting knives, forks, and spoons into the drawer.

Another thought had her chewing on her bottom lip. Jon was too willing to jump in head first when danger threatened. Going against the DiNardo family could get him hurt. Or worse. As safe as she felt when she was with him, living in her house put him in danger. She'd been an idiot for going along with him acting like her boyfriend.

She looked up and there he was, standing in the doorway, broad shoulders filling it, not looking scared or even the least bit concerned. "He drove off."

"Okay." She let out the breath she'd been holding in a rush. "I've made a mistake."

He raised a brow. "We all make them."

"No, really. I shouldn't have involved you."

"Too late."

His offhanded attitude did nothing to ease the dread tying her stomach in knots. "No, it's not. I never should've rented the apartment to you. You need to leave."

He moved into the kitchen. "I'm not going anywhere."

"You don't understand. That guy got out of prison a few days ago. He's dangerous. I'm revoking your lease. I'll give you back your deposit."

"You're spooked. Tell me what's going on."

"He's an ex-boyfriend, and he's nuts. Or at least I think he is. You need to leave," she repeated, this time with more urgency.

He stood there watching her patiently, his expression saying he wasn't going anywhere. Rane gripped the counter, her temper beginning to simmer. "Look. You don't have a choice. We made it look like we're together. He'll get jealous. I can't rent to you any longer."

Cooper came in through the dog door, and she bent to lock it. He brushed his head against Jon's leg, and he reached down to scratch behind Cooper's ears.

"I'm not leaving." He tone made it clear—case closed.

She stifled a groan of frustration. If he went all army strong on her things could, and probably would, go from bad to disastrous.

"Tell me what's going on," he repeated.

She stood straight and looked him in the eye to make the lies more credible. "Like I said, he's an ex-boyfriend. He can get jealous. It would be better all-around if you moved out. I'm really sorry for the trouble."

"Not a chance, sweetheart." He turned and opened the door to the fridge.

"What are you doing?" She said each word carefully, her patience thinning like an overstretched rubber band.

"Seeing what's for dinner." He pulled out a container, holding it up to inspect the contents. "What's this?"

She walked up and jerked the glass bowl out of his hand. "Chicken." She shoved it back into the fridge, slamming the door shut. "Let's go. We'll go up to your apartment and I'll help you get anything you've unpacked back into boxes. I'm not feeding you dinner."

When she would've opened the kitchen door he shifted in front of her and gently held her arms. She wondered if the army had trained him to move so fluidly.

"No. We're making dinner. From your dining table we can keep an eye on the street. I want to see if he drives by again."

"Why are you doing this? You're crazy."

"Not crazy. There's no way I'm walking away when you're in danger."

She rolled her eyes. "Oh, please. It's you who's in danger."

"I'm sticking. Get used to it." He turned back to the fridge and took out the chicken and set it on the counter. He fished around in the vegetable drawer. Tomato, lettuce, and an onion joined the chicken. "Do you have tortillas?"

"You really are insane. This isn't your fight. You aren't in Afghanistan anymore."

Eyes steely, he responded, "Sweetheart, if I was in Afghanistan that guy would be face first in the dirt with an M-sixteen pointed at his head." He waited a beat. "Tortillas?"

***

Jon watched out of the corner of his eye as Rane raised her hands to her head as if she was keeping it from exploding. She spoke through clenched teeth, her words clipped. "I'm getting changed. I want you gone when I come back down. Come on, Cooper."

The dog looked at him with what Jon thought was guy-to-guy understanding before following her out. He opened the fridge again and after some more rummaging found corn tortillas and a brick of Monterey Jack cheese in the deli drawer.

While concerned, he had to admit, he felt pleased. It wasn't only that something was happening—the case was bearing fruit— it was the back and forth with Rane. He bet she didn't know how expressive her face was. Her expression had held dead-on sincerity, but her eyes told him she was holding back. She was scared, and yet she'd tried to kick him out. He'd give her an "A" for guts, but no way was she forcing him out.

Something was off about her relationship with Kyle DiNardo and he didn't like it. Even if he hadn't known about the narcotics angle, Jon would've recognized she was lying, or at least not telling the whole truth about their involvement.

Within a day of meeting her, he knew she wasn't criminally involved. She might as well have the word "integrity" tattooed on her forehead. There was no hiding it was part of her basic makeup. Her genuine worry and sadness over kids dying from heroin overdoses was clearly heartfelt. Trying to figure all the angles, he grabbed a cutting board and began chopping a tomato.

Twenty minutes later she walked back into the kitchen. He didn't react to her appearance, but she sure did it for him.

She wore stretchy knee-length black pants and a snug fitting, long-sleeved t-shirt. He wondered if she knew how well it molded to her slender build, outlining curves in all the right places. Her hair was pulled back in a ponytail, and her bangs brushed her large sea-green eyes. When she leaned against the doorframe with her arms crossed and gaze narrowed, he had a hard time not scooping her up to see how she tasted.

The sparks in her eyes made him cautious about turning his back to her. "You hungry?"

"Yes."

"Great. Tacos are almost ready. Good thing you had chicken already cooked. Made it easy."

"So happy to accommodate."

He ignored the sarcasm. "You want to get the plates and flatware?"

When she continued scowling, he paused. "Look, sweetheart, you need to eat. I need to eat. There's nothing in the refrigerator upstairs. I want to be down here to keep an eye out for that guy. Next time you can come up to my apartment and I'll spring for the food."

She tapped a fist against her forehead in exasperation. "This isn't about the food, army, and I can keep an eye out myself. He's my problem. I'll call the police if I see him again. And stop calling me sweetheart."

He laughed. "Right now you are my sweetheart, but don't think it's personal. This could be an easy fix. If this guy thinks you're with me he might leave you alone."

"Or he could go off the deep end. He's dangerous. I told you, I don't want you involved. You could get hurt."

When he gave her a blank look she threw up her hands. "God save me from alpha males who want to play hero." She stalked to the drawer and pulled out utensils.

He took out the pinto beans from the microwave. Seeing that some of them had exploded, he got a sponge. He didn't want to give her anything else to yell at him about so he wiped up the bean guts. He flipped the tortillas warming in a skillet before eyeing her again.

From her expression, she was waging a furious mental debate over what to do about him.

He needed her to tell him what she knew about the DiNardo organization, but he couldn't push. She was smart and would become suspicious. Or get really serious about kicking him out.

He waited until she'd finished her tacos and was sipping from a glass of wine before he brought the conversation back around to Kyle DiNardo. Not that talking to her was a hardship. She was quick-witted, made interesting observations about people, and society in general, and when she wasn't pissed at him, she was sweet and funny.

She pushed her plate back and moved restlessly in her chair, her gaze fixed on the street. He knew it was time, but he needed to tread lightly. He couldn't divulge what he knew, but he needed to find out if she had any information that would lead him and his team to evidence they could use to prosecute the DiNardos.

"Tell me about the ex. What's his name?"

She worried her bottom lip, then sighed. "Kyle."

"Last name?"

"Nope. I don't want you to Google him."

Smart girl. "Why are you afraid of him?"

She shrugged. "When he got out of prison, I thought he'd leave me alone. I didn't think he'd hurt me, but since he was out there tonight, and that was probably him trying to get into my house the other night, I've got to presume he's up to something. I'll call his parole officer in the morning."

"Good plan. What was he in for?"

The look she gave him didn't make sense. She almost looked guilty. Jon took a mental step back. Something wasn't adding up here. Maybe she'd really been in love with the guy. She leaned forward to pick up her plate and he reached for her hand. "The dishes can wait. What was he in for?"

She tugged her hand free and went back to looking out the window. "Possession with intent to distribute. He'd been in for three years."

"What drug?"

"Heroin."

"How'd you get mixed up with the guy?"

She picked up her wine glass but didn't drink, instead twirling it by the stem. "I knew him in high school. He was different then. Fun, easy going. He told me what his family did but swore he wasn't getting sucked into that. The summer after graduation we started dating. I went away to college, but saw him when I came back home."

"Was he ever violent?"

"Yeah. During the summer after my sophomore year of college I tried to end it. He went crazy, broke things. But he didn't hurt me."

"Were the police involved?"

"No, only my dad. He got in Kyle's face, told him to stay away from me. I went back to college and tried to forget about him."

The heroin was the connection, and Jon tried to think if there was a link to Rane. "Were you involved with him at the time he was sent to prison?"

She shrugged. "Not really. After I graduated he wanted to get back together, but I knew he'd gotten involved in the drug business. He had money, lots of money, but didn't have a job."

"That's a pretty good tip-off. What happened?"

"He got caught." She broke eye contact and looked down at her wine, then back up. "Now he's on parole and was outside my house an hour ago."

He wondered what she was holding back. "Tell me about him. Does he have family in Seattle? How would he get a car? Where would he stay?"

Rane shook her head. "What are you going to do? Go find him and beat him up?"

He looked at her thoughtfully. "No. But the more I know the better prepared I'll be. I agree that was probably him the other night. Being prepared is a good idea."

"Prepared for what? Kyle isn't your problem."

"He became my problem when he knocked you down."

She lifted her hands and then let them fall. "He was running away, and I was in his path. That was my fault as much as his."

He didn't bother to respond, and she blew out a breath that fluttered her bangs. He figured she didn't believe that either.

"Look," she said. "When I came home after I graduated from college a friend came to visit me. Kyle showed up at my apartment and Jordan was there. They had words. That evening when Jordan was walking out to his car he was jumped and had the crap beaten out of him. "I'm sure it was Kyle."

"Was he arrested?"

She shook her head, eyes shadowed. "He knocked him down from behind. Jordan never got a good look at him. He ended up with a broken nose and a couple cracked ribs. But I know it was Kyle." Her expression clouded. "You see? That's why you need to leave. Kyle won't hurt me, but he might go after you."

"I can take care of myself, and I wouldn't bet on him not hurting you."

She didn't respond, and he wasn't going to grill her. He got up and brought his plate to the sink. She followed, and together they cleaned up the dinner dishes. She was subdued, and although she tried to hide it, he could tell she was worried. When it became obvious she was waiting for him to leave, he decided to meet the opposition head on.

"I'm sleeping on your couch tonight."

"What? Why?" She dropped her fork and it clattered to the floor. He'd never seen her flustered before.

"Sweetheart, this guy could be stalking you. He tried your windows the other night and parked outside your house today. I'll sleep on the couch to be here if he tries anything."

"I'll be fine. I'll call the cops if he shows up again."

He was shaking his head before she'd finished talking. "Not good enough. This guy could cause a shitload of trouble before the police arrive. Get me a blanket and a pillow. I'll bunk on the couch, and you'll never notice I'm here."

"What about tomorrow night? Or the night after? You can't sleep on my couch every night."

He bit back the comment he wanted to make about being happier sleeping in her bed, but not saying it did nothing to erase the mental image of her naked body beneath his. He coughed to clear his throat. "We'll deal with tonight first."

She looked like she was going to say something, but she shook her head and climbed the stairs, back straight. Minutes later she returned with her arms full. Pushing the bedding at him, she turned back to the stairs like she was going to leave without saying anything, but checked herself, and turned back. "Look, it's not like I don't appreciate you looking out for me, but I'm not helpless. I have thought through what I'd do if Kyle came back and threatened me."

"What'd you come up with?"

"I'll shoot him."

***

Rane lay under the covers hoping to fall asleep. She had to admit that having Jon downstairs on the couch made her feel safe. Warm. Protected. If he hadn't been there she would have spent the night listening to the old house settling, obsessing over every small sound. Cooper yawned from his bed by the wall, and she turned onto her side and let her eyes drift shut.

Early the next morning, she sat at the little breakfast table in the kitchen, toast and coffee in front of her as she swiped through the news on her iPad. Jon had left sometime before she'd gotten up. The bedding was folded neatly at the end of the couch with the pillow on top, and there was already made hot coffee, which was an unexpected pleasure.

She wondered if he suspected there was more to what had happened with Kyle than she'd told him. There were things she'd never told anyone about her father. The cop who had set up Kyle to take the fall and get him out of his daughter's life.

Even though it never sat well with her, she'd do whatever it took to protect her dad.

Chapter Four

"So you think she knows more than she's letting on?" Jon looked at his brother sitting across the table from him. They shared the Garretson family's strong features, but instead of their father's blue, his brother inherited their mother's dark green eyes. They both had light brown hair that streaked blond in the summer.

"Yeah, definitely. She knew him for several years, right about the time his family took control of the pipeline into Canada."

"Maybe she's dirty. She could have dealt for them. Made a little extra on the side."

"No way, Nate."

His brow raised, Nathan eyed him, considering. "Seem pretty sure of that, JonJon. You've spent what? A couple weeks with her? Think you've got her figured out?"

"She's clean. I'm not saying she told me all she knows, but she's never been involved with the drug operation."

Nathan sat for a moment taking in what Jon told him. "Okay. Assume you're right. For now. What else you got?"

Jon reached for his coffee. "You remember Kyle DiNardo's arresting officer?"

"Yeah, wasn't it Smith?" Jon could see his brother do the mental check. "Rane Smith. Connection?"

"I saw a photo of Doug Smith in her house. He's her dad."

"Shit. How did we not know that?"

"You tell me, detective."

Nathan bit into a slice of bacon. "Smith is a common name and since we didn't know about Rane's link to DiNardo until about a month ago, I didn't put it together." He grinned. "Neither did you, bro."

"Yeah. She'd told me her dad was a cop but I didn't realize who he was."

The brothers met for breakfast at the diner a block from the police station. Jon knew it was unusual to be on the same task force, but he was grateful he had his brother to bounce things off of, especially when it came to drug trafficking. The DiNardo family had been square in the team's sights for a while. The brothers hadn't and wouldn't ever tell the rest of the team, or their boss, that there was a personal element to this case. The Garretsons had a score to settle with the head of the family, Simon DiNardo.

Jon smeared butter on his pancakes, then said, "I didn't expect Kyle to show up last night. Especially after I chased him off a few days ago."

Nathan's jaw tensed. "You could've put a bullet through his head. It would've saved everyone a lot of grief."

"Gotta say, revenge would be sweet."

"Yeah." Nathan looked at his brother. "He deserves it."

"We'll get him, Nate. He'll pay for what he did to Savannah. But we'll do it right."

Nathan nodded. Savannah's death had propelled his brother into joining the police force. Hell, it was probably what had set Jon on that path too.

Savannah Montague, brainy, funny, and full of life. She and Nathan had begun dating during their second year at the state university, and his brother had fallen hard. What nobody knew was Savannah was self-medicating to offset the stress of being an overachieving straight-A student. She'd gone from Adderall to cocaine, and then to heroin to slow down the hyper she got from the cocaine.

Two weeks before college graduation she'd overdosed. Jon would never forget the call after Nathan had found his girlfriend's body.

After clearing the PD's probationary period, Nathan worked hard and focused on joining the narcotics unit. Once on board, his investigations revealed the half arrow mark on the little bag he'd found next to Savannah's body belonged to the DiNardo family. It didn't take long to learn Kyle DiNardo had been her dealer.

Simon was a careful man. He managed his family's business by running the drug money through legitimate operations. He made sure his hands and his books were always clean. But Nathan was tireless.

When Jon joined the force, he followed in his brother's footsteps, working hard to get noticed. When he joined the narcotics unit, he partnered with Nate to carefully craft the case against the DiNardo family. A lot of what they had was circumstantial. What they needed was direct, incontrovertible evidence tying Simon and Kyle directly to the heroin overdoses plaguing the city. The DA wouldn't go after such a large crime syndicate unless he was as close to a slam-dunk as he could get.

Nathan leaned back in his seat. "How'd you know it was Kyle sitting in a car outside Rane's house last night?"

Jon stretched his legs under the table. "I used my great detecting powers, which also helped me avoid Rane pepper spraying me twice in the last couple days."

Nathan chuckled. "She tried to pepper spray you?"

"Both times I was sitting on the porch waiting for her. She walks up and next thing you know she's got the little canister in her hand and a finger on the pump."

"You always had the smoothest moves, bro."

"Yeah, well those smooth moves got her to tell me it was Kyle in the car. She's jumpy, man. I spent the night on her couch and kept an eye out. I didn't want the fucker breaking in and getting to her."

Nathan eyed him. "Don't get a thing for her, little brother. You're on the job."

Jon took his time chewing a mouthful of pancake before replying, "Too late for that."

Nathan sat back in his chair, his expression hardening. "Fuck. This woman is a suspect."

Jon shook his head. "I told you, she's not. She doesn't want me to get involved. In fact, she tried to break the lease. She's afraid I'll get hurt." Nate's brow went up. "She's ticked 'cause I won't budge." Jon looked his brother in the eye. "Don't worry. Even though I have a thing for her, it doesn't mean shit. I'll do what I always do. My job."

"JonJon, we've got to get you out of there. To hell with the cover. You get emotionally involved and you lose your objectivity. Then you'll both be in danger."

"You're talking like my brother, not a cop. We went to all that trouble of getting me established in the apartment above her house. I'm seeing this through. I'm not leaving her to deal with this guy on her own. I won't mess up the operation."

Nathan leaned back, pinching the bridge of his nose, then he looked across the table. "Okay. But watch yourself."

"Yeah."

They paid for their breakfast and walked out into the crisp morning. Nice weather was holding and puffy white clouds moved across a sky of endless blue.

"I'll follow up on the plate number you gave me. See whose car DiNardo was driving. Keep working on Rane. Get her to tell you more about what our boy was doing when she was dating him."

Jon nodded and started walking toward the parking lot where he'd left his truck. Nathan turned toward the station, then called out. "JonJon, you better get the little hearts out of your eyes, man. It's embarrassing."

Jon didn't bother responding. He flipped up his middle finger and kept walking, his brother's laughter echoing in his ears.

Chapter Five

Rane let herself into her house through the kitchen door, fumbling with the deadbolt as she twisted it. She entered the alarm code with shaking fingers, swearing silently when she had to reenter the number twice. Cooper had to go out. She wanted to keep him near, but forced herself to unlock the flap in the backdoor for him. She sank to the floor with her back against the door, wrapping her arms around her knees and resting her forehead on her arms. She was home and she was safe, though safe was a relative term, looser in its connotation than it'd been an hour ago.

Cooper nosed his way back through the dog door. He licked her chin and she wrapped an arm around him and buried her face in his fur, working on steadying her breathing until she felt she'd gained a slippery grasp on her ability to control the shaking wracking her body. She hadn't even brought in her groceries. They were still in the trunk of her car. She'd get them eventually. She had to give herself time to regroup.

Jon's truck hadn't been in the driveway. Not that it would've mattered if it was.

She replayed the events of the past hour in her head and was as horrified now as she'd been while it was happening.

On her way home from work, she'd stopped at the grocery store. She'd worked overtime, and it'd been after nine when she left the hospital. Her fridge was empty, and she needed to buy groceries, so she headed to her favorite supermarket. She was pushing her cart through the aisles of the brightly lit store, only half paying attention to what she was putting in the basket.

That she was perusing a boxed brownie mix should've been a clue she was seeking comfort after a killer shift. The heroin ODs were still coming. A couple months ago maybe they'd get one a week. Now, they were getting one, sometimes two a day.

With the brownie mix in her basket, she wondered if Jon was home this evening. He probably had a date. Well, good for him. She bet he didn't have trust issues. He was probably out with some pretty girl-next-door type. They'd fall madly in love, get married, buy a house in the 'burbs, have two kids, a boy and a girl, and both would have their dad's sun-streaked hair and gorgeous eyes.

She was making herself miserable.

Okay. He was hot. There. She admitted it to herself. There were plenty of hot guys in Seattle. But Jon made her heart flip in her chest every time she saw him. Acknowledging how she felt didn't mean she'd do anything about it. She couldn't date him. Ever. Given the Kyle situation, seeing anyone was too dangerous. Best to keep avoiding Jon and hope her stupid heart would get over itself.

She'd paid for her groceries and wheeled her cart out to her car. Heavy clouds hung low from the dark sky, and the temperature had dropped since she'd left the hospital. She'd bent over to place her bagged groceries in her trunk. That's where she'd made her mistake, turning her back to the parking lot as she'd leaned in to push the bags further back.

A prickling of the small hairs at the back of her neck had her straightening abruptly and turning around, her heart jumping into her throat. Two men stood behind her. Their stance and the way they were looking at her screamed they weren't offering to take her cart. One was tall and muscular, the other short and stocky. The tall one had a shaved head that gleamed under the diffused light coming from the pole she'd intentionally parked next to. They weren't dressed like hired goons, but she knew that's what they were.

The shorter man spoke. "Rane Smith, Mr. DiNardo wishes to speak with you."

"No." Panic had her nerves jumping. She backed up, her legs bumping against her car. Her car had keyless entry so she didn't even have her keys in her hand to put between her fingers as a weapon. Her gaze darted around. A woman was getting into a car about five rows over, but other than that, the parking lot was empty.

"You're not in danger, Ms. Smith. Mr. DiNardo simply wants a conversation."

His comment that she wasn't in danger was belied by a gun holstered at his waist he'd revealed when he put his hands on his hips. She didn't think the show and tell was accidental.

He pointed to the dark SUV parked next to her car. "Mr. DiNardo is in the driver's seat of that vehicle. You'll sit in the front passenger seat, and when the conversation is over, you'll be free to leave."

She glanced at the SUV. She hadn't paid any attention to it, but now it looked dark and sinister. The back windows were tinted, and she couldn't see the driver. Her mind raced for a way to stall, looking for an opportunity to get herself to safety. Her purse hung heavily on her shoulder.

"How do I know he won't drive off with me in the car?"

"You have my word. Ms. Smith, you need to get in the vehicle."

She deliberately looked over his shoulder. "Cops are here."

They weren't, but both men looked. She took her chance and darted between the cars. The tall guy was quick and grabbed her from behind. Rane sucked in a breath to scream as a huge hand clamped over her mouth. Twisting and turning, she tried to bite him but couldn't open her mouth. The best she could do was to kick him in the shin. The short guy tried to assist his partner, and she blasted him in the face with the pepper spray she'd managed to snatch from the side pocket of her purse.

He reeled back, wheezing out a string of profanity, but Rane's reprieve was momentary. Big guy hit her hand with a vicious side chop and sent the little can of spray skittering on the asphalt.

In a blur of motion, he opened the door and he bundled her into the SUV. He threw the purse she'd dropped in after her, then slammed the door. She grappled for the handle as the locks clicked to engage. She was breathing in ragged breaths when she whipped around to face the man in the driver's seat.

"Hello, Rane."

She stared at Simon DiNardo's pale complexion. She suppressed a shudder, suddenly feeling cold down to her marrow. "Let me go."

"Calm down. I'm not going to hurt you as long as you cooperate."

She drew a deep breath, held it for a moment, then let it out. She'd expected Kyle, but instead his scary as shit brother sat with one hand resting on the steering wheel like they were catching up on old times.

As much as she'd dreaded Kyle's return from prison, Simon's presence was way more alarming. Her mind pinballed to a night during her senior year of high school when Kyle had shown up at their meeting place, a little park a couple blocks from her house. His face was bloody and his body bruised.

He'd told his brother he didn't want anything to do with the family business, and in return, Simon had nearly killed him. Simon took Kyle's announcement as a sign of disrespect to the family and its business. Loyalty to family was more important than anything, and Simon had beaten it into his brother until Kyle towed the line.

"What do you want?" She tried to school her voice not to reveal that she was scared beyond reason but didn't think she fooled him for a minute.

From the light shining through the windshield, she could see him fairly well. In his early-forties, Simon DiNardo clearly worked at being forgettable. He was dressed in dad jeans with a tan jacket over a button-down shirt. He wore his brown hair trimmed short and parted on the side in a conservative cut. His appearance was so unremarkable he would easily blend into a crowd unnoticed.

He turned his head to look at her and a shudder rippled through her. His eyes. She remembered those eyes. The irises were the palest gray and were so light they nearly blended with the white sclera. She knew what she'd felt as a teenager was true.

She was looking into the face of evil.

"What do you want?"

Simon leaned back in his seat. "That depends on you, Rane." He gave her a lipless smile that made her think of a snake. "I'm concerned about my little brother."

"I don't have anything to do with your brother. If you'd both leave me alone we'd have nothing to talk about."

He shifted to face her more fully and she saw an ugly scar stretching from his temple to curl under his left ear. It hadn't been there years ago, the last time she'd seen him. The scar looked like it hadn't healed properly and was puckered and uneven. She wondered who had done it, and was sorry they hadn't finished the job. "We have plenty to talk about since my family has a score to settle with yours."

Everything inside Rane froze to icy stillness. For a fleeting moment, she wished desperately that Jon were with her. He made her feel safe. "I don't know what you're talking about."

"I think you do. Your family owes mine." He stared at her with those unblinking, soulless eyes. "I have an offer that could help settle the balance."

"My family owes you nothing. I want out of this car." Futilely, she pulled on the door handle. She didn't know where the goons were, or, if she managed to get out of the car, whether they'd be there to grab her again. She could barely think past the thundering sound of blood in her ears.

Simon tapped his fingers on the steering wheel, and she saw his eyes moving as he scanned the parking lot before returning his attention to her. "Your father set up Kyle. You let him do it. Both of you should be in prison, but it was my brother who paid the price for lusting after you."

Her mind reeled at his words, and she could admit to a tiny amount of relief. Simon petrified her, but at least what she feared he'd learn was out in the open. "There was more to it than that."

"Not for me, and certainly not for Kyle. You and your father broke the law. Police detective Douglas Smith set up Kyle because daddy didn't want a DiNardo touching his little girl. You let your father do it. You protected him, and now you're going to pay."

As scared as she was, she was also pissed off. "Kyle should've been in prison. He was dealing. He'd been screwing another girl while he was seeing me. That girl died and Kyle killed her. It wasn't your heroin that did her in, she'd been strangled. When my father found out, he did what he thought he had to do, he protected me."

Simon's thin smile made Rane nauseous. "Such a sweet sentiment. But your father planted heroin in my brother's car, and then the detective lied in court. You knew about it and didn't come forward. That makes you both guilty."

"You don't know that. You have no evidence of what my father did, and you have no idea what I knew."

Pale gray eyes regarded her as if he could see through her. She wondered if he would strike with the speed of a snake. "I have all the evidence I need. I visited him yesterday."

She stared at him numbly, the icy chill clinging to her bones. "You went to see my dad?"

"I'm his cousin from Portland. Can't you see the family resemblance?" He turned his horrible face toward her and grinned. "He was happy for the company and couldn't shut up. On and on he rambled like an idiot until he got to the part about planting the heroin in Kyle's car. Then cousin Dougie let his dirty deed slip. Said you weren't happy when you found out. Got it all on my phone."

She couldn't believe the nurses let Simon into the facility. Her poor father hadn't a clue who he was talking to.

"Good girl Rane didn't let the DA's office know what her father had done. You let my brother spend three years in prison."

Partially true, but it didn't absolve her, and she knew it. "He'd already served a year by the time I found out."

"When you found out doesn't matter. He wasn't guilty of the crime he was charged with."

"But he was guilty of hundreds of others, including murdering that girl."

Simon's voice became more menacing. "Tell me Rane, what would you do to keep your old man from dying in a prison psych ward? There are so many dangerous people there. I wouldn't be surprised if one of them...I don't know, stabbed him and he bled out in his chair while watching cartoons." He sneered. "If you want to protect him and stay out of prison yourself, you'll do what I want."

"He's been diagnosed with Alzheimer's," she hissed. "No one would believe that recording."

Simon shrugged. "I'm not without influence."

Rane had gotten so cold she began to shiver, and she wondered if she'd shatter into jagged shards of ice before Simon let her go. Or killed her. "I'm not doing anything for you."

"Your choice, of course. But you might want to think about it. You won't like living in a six by eight cage."

No, she wouldn't. But she'd do it to keep her father alive and well. As if Simon would let her Dad live.

"Even if I did what you wanted, how do I know you'll keep your word?"

"You don't. But I'll give it anyway."

Rane looked across the parking lot where a woman pushed a shopping cart out of the store, a toddler in the front seat. Those goons were somewhere outside the SUV, one of them, probably both of them, had guns. That kind of threat would be ever-present for the rest of her life because of the decision she'd made not to expose her father.

She made herself ask, "What do you want me to do?"

Simon nodded his head as if he'd known she'd come around. "The man who's renting your apartment is named Jon Garretson."

Rane frowned. "No, it's Jon Davidson."

"That's his cover. His name is Jon Garretson and he's a detective with Seattle PD. He's on a task force that's been investigating me and my family for years. You're going to find out what he knows and pass that information along to me."

Rane's hand gripped the armrest as she shook her head. "You're wrong."

"No, I'm not. Garretson's a cop and so is his brother. They're on the same task force. Jon was assigned to watch you. They've been dogging me for too long and I'm done with it."

For her it was a no-brainer. Simon wasn't really a human being and she knew she could trust Jon. He'd protected her. "I don't believe you."

Simon shrugged. "You'll find out for yourself once you do as I say."

"No."

He sighed like a teacher disappointed by his prize pupil. "So brave, yet so misguided." He leaned toward her. "You'll do exactly what I ask because you don't want your father to die in a prison psych ward, and you don't want to go to prison yourself. You don't want your dog hurt, or your friend Lily to drown in the pool at her condo. You don't want to get shot when you're sitting at a stop light on your way to work. Shall I go on?"

When he paused the night seemed to pulse against the windows of the SUV. The images he'd put in her head were too horrible to imagine. His eerie pale eyes glowed faintly in the muted light. "Are we clear?"

Rane stared at him, her mind stuck on the horrific images his words had conjured.

"Rane. Are we clear?"

She nodded jerkily before asking, "What does Kyle think of your plan?"

Simon's blank expression didn't waver. "You leave my little brother to me. You deal with the cop."

"I don't see why you think he'll tell me anything. He's my tenant."

"Lure him in like you did Kyle. I'm guessing the cop will be all over you in a heartbeat if you give him the go-ahead."

She wanted to vomit. She wanted to kill Simon DiNardo where he sat.

She wanted to cry.

"Act the frightened female and play on his hero instincts. You'll be surprised how easy it'll be to get him to talk." Simon handed her a card. "That's my cell number. Call only if you have something. I'll be in touch. And Rane, don't think the cops are the only ones with their eyes on you. If I get reports you aren't moving ahead with my plan, I have plenty of ways to motivate you."

The door locks clicked and Rane scrambled out of that car like her life depended on it.

***

Rane moved mechanically around her kitchen. She'd forced herself to retrieve her groceries from her car and piled them on the counter. Searching for something normal to do, she emptied a can of soup into a pan and set it on the stove, then started putting away the groceries. Cooper lay curled by the table, his eyes following her every move. When Jon's truck roared up the driveway she paused, standing stock-still while her mind raced.

She still didn't know what to do about him. She didn't want to believe what Simon had told her, but he'd made a sick kind of sense. Jon was hyper alert and had a gun. Sure, he'd been in the military, but if he was training to be a firefighter, he wouldn't need a sidearm. She almost laughed. She'd told him he'd make a good cop.

Hard rapping at the kitchen door had her lowering the flame under the soup.

"Rane. Open the door." The harsh sound of Jon's voice accompanied more pounding, this time with what sounded like his fist.

She opened the door, and before she could take a breath he was in the kitchen, closing the door with his foot, backing her up against the wall. "Are you okay?" His hands were moving up and down her arms as if checking for broken bones. He smelled like the night, wild and dark.

When she stared at him mutely he must have read the fear in her eyes. "Fuck this," he growled. He cupped her face, his long fingers spearing into her hair. He tipped her head up, then caught her mouth with his in a scorching kiss. She felt so cold, his lips burned hers. The ice that had gripped her since her meeting with Simon cracked, and she felt a flood of sensation. Attraction, anger, desire all fueled a combustive combination that set her off.

She brought her hands up to fist in his hair. With the wall at her back, he leaned into her until they were melded together from lips to knees. She tensed her arms, meaning to push him away, but instead found her fingers tightening in his hair, neither pushing him away nor pulling him closer.

His tongue slipped past her lips to slide against hers. The heat flaring between them was painful as it reached into her bones. Finally, she gave in and her grip relaxed, her hand slipping under the collar of his shirt to feel the heat of his skin, which warmed her fingers. He braced his hands on the wall on either side of her, his head bent to brush his mouth along her jaw.

Rane fought to maintain a hold on the maddening explosion of desire. She lowered her hands to his arms and felt muscles tense in response. Pushing against him was like pushing against a granite wall. Finally he eased back, taking a deep breath before pressing his lips to her forehead. He pulled away and the stark passion on his face nearly undid her.

"Jon."

His eyes darkened and his fingers moved back to her hair, brushing it back from her face. She thought he was making a monumental effort to contain whatever emotions consumed him.

"Okay, okay. Sorry." He stepped back until they were no longer touching, lifting his hands up as if to show he wasn't a threat. "I didn't mean to come on so strong."

The chills returned without the comfort of his body heat. "Then why did you?" She frowned as realization hit. "You know what happened. How?"

His expression tightened, and indecision crossed his face.

"Well?"

"You don't make it easy for a guy, do you?"

"I won't make it easy for you."

His gaze narrowed. "What's that supposed to mean?" When she didn't say anything, remaining motionless with her back against the wall, he raised his brows. "Rane?"

"Are you a cop?"

The truth flickered of his eyes and was gone in an instant.

"Whoa. Where did that come from?"

"Answer the question. Are you a cop? Is your name really Jon Garretson?"

He stared at her for a long minute until finally nodding. "Yes to both."

Rane bit back a sigh. Lesson learned. Anger burned through her, at herself, at him. She'd believed him, trusted him, and once again she learned trusting someone only led to pain.

She stepped past him, and picked up a spoon to stir the soup bubbling on the stove. "You're here to spy on me. Apparently, you're good at it since you found out what happened tonight."

"The team had you under surveillance when you left the hospital." His words sounded like they were being bitten off one at a time. "The two guys watching you made the call to let it play out. If DiNardo had tried to take off with you in the SUV, they were prepared to stop him."

"I see. No harm, no foul. Me being terrified didn't matter as long as you got what you needed to make your case."

"Hell no." She glanced over to see him jamming his fingers through his hair. "Some members of the team think you're working with the DiNardos."

"I see. It's nice to know where I stand."

"I know you're not. I trust you."

She turned, raising her brows. "That's why you've lied to me since the moment we first met. Everything about you has been a lie."

"Maybe at the start, but the situation has changed."

"Oh, really. How has it changed?"

"It just has."

"Right. It doesn't matter. You should go. You need to get packing because you're being evicted."

Chapter Six

"I'm not going anywhere."

Jon moved toward Rane and she backed up a step. He hated that he'd put that wariness on her face. She tossed the spoon into the sink with a clatter. "Don't you come near me, Jon *Garretson*. You may trust me, but I don't trust you. You lied. You told me you'd been in Afghanistan and were training to be a firefighter."

He stepped back cautiously. He'd treated unexploded IEDs with as much care. This situation didn't feel all that different. One wrong move and everything could blow up in his face. "I was in Afghanistan. That part's true. Clearly, I'm not training to be a firefighter."

"Because you're a cop. You're undercover, and you've been watching me."

"Yeah, I'm a cop. I *was* undercover. Obviously my cover's been blown to hell."

"So why all the drama when you came in? That was a pretty good act, by the way. Very convincing."

He wanted to shake her, make her understand something he wasn't even sure he understood himself. He'd been pulled to her from the first moment he'd seen her through the screen door. He'd never suspected she could make him lose control of emotions he'd carefully guarded all his life.

Panic had ripped through him when he'd gotten the call from Nate. "No act. I got word you'd been nabbed by Simon DiNardo, and that you were talking to him."

"Yeah, so?"

"So? Jesus, Rane. That guy's psychotic. You were. . .are in danger."

"I was, and your guys knew about it and let it happen," she choked out. "I handled it. I don't need you."

He watched as she shut down, as her warm expressive eyes turned blank. "Now that I know who and what you really are, and that you've been lying to me, you don't need to pretend we're friends. You certainly don't need to act like you're attracted to me." She gave a self-deprecating laugh. "That was a jerk move, by the way, kissing me like it meant something." When she turned back to the stove she moved carefully, as if she were fragile enough to shatter. She turned off the burner and got a single bowl from the cupboard.

"It did mean something. You mean something. There's nothing dishonest about my feelings for you."

She paid an undue amount of attention to ladling soup into the bowl. "Now that I know, at least have the decency to be truthful with me. You needed to get close to me for your case. You rented my apartment to that end, then chased away bad guys under the guise of a little-more-than-friendly tenant. All that was a lie. You storming in, kissing me brainless was you being honest? You'll have to excuse me if I think that's bullshit."

He could feel the ground eroding beneath him. He'd lost control of the situation when it had become significantly more dangerous. When she set the bowl on the table and took a seat, he pulled out the chair across from her, turning it around to straddle it. He'd try for cool and rational.

"Rane." He waited until she raised her gaze to his. "My name is Jonathan David Garretson. I'm a detective with the Seattle PD. I'm on a task force investigating the source of the heroin flooding the streets. The same heroin that's killing the users showing up in your ER."

"Have you determined I'm not the source of that heroin?"

He couldn't see past the filter she put over her expression. Her face remained unnaturally expressionless, the warmth in her eyes replaced by a distance he couldn't reach. She'd closed herself off behind a wall he couldn't get through.

"You were never suspected as the source of the heroin."

She swallowed a spoonful of soup. "Well, that's comforting."

He propped his elbows on the back of his seat, running his hands through his hair in frustration. She was turning the guilt screws real tight. "I'm here because of your connection to the DiNardo family. They're the ones bringing the heroin into the city. We believe Simon

DiNardo is distributing to the dealers, but we haven't been able to pin him to it yet."

"So you thought I would be able to help you with that?"

"We knew Kyle DiNardo had written to you when he was in prison, that you two had been together, and that he still has a thing for you."

"You read the letters he sent me."

He nodded. "We got a warrant and intercepted the letters, then resealed the envelopes and sent them on to you. Even though he'd stopped writing, Kyle was getting out and we figured he'd try to contact you.

"The DiNardos are tight and you were our best avenue to get to the family. If Kyle started coming around here I was supposed to hang with him, share a beer. Let him know I was interested in hooking up with some dope. Maybe even in dealing for him."

"I see. Too bad it didn't work out the way you'd planned. Why did you chase him off that night? And then act like you were my boyfriend? That doesn't make sense."

"I wasn't sure it was him that night. Acting like your boyfriend wasn't what I'd intended. When I realized you were scared of him I modified the plan."

"I see." She rose, picking up the bowl and taking it to the sink, and dumped the contents down the drain. She'd hardly eaten any of it. She turned to face him. "I think you should go. I'm tired." The wall she'd put up between them had crumbled a bit, and he could see her fear. Of course, she was scared. He'd deal with that in a minute, but first he needed to find out what Simon had said.

"Sorry, but I need more information. Tell me about your meeting with Simon. What did he want?"

"Nothing. I'm going upstairs. Lock the door behind you when you leave."

She walked past him. "Rane, wait." He reached for her arm as she brushed past him.

She whirled, temper finally breaking through. Jon was glad to see the show of emotion, even though it wasn't the one he wanted.

"No, I won't wait. You got what you were after. You fooled me, and meant to use me. I'm done with you." She pulled free from his grip.

"You've got to talk to me."

"No, I don't." She turned away from him and went upstairs.

***

In flannel pants and a tank top, Rane descended the staircase rubbing her eyes. Cooper trailed behind her. Today her shift didn't start until eleven, but still she'd woken early, her mind immediately full of the events of the previous night. Despite everything that had happened, what kept popping up in her head was that senseless, mind-numbing kiss. Jon had sure made it feel real. The worst part was her response. She'd practically climbed him like a tree. Knowing that his "passion" was part of his undercover assignment made her cringe.

She almost tripped on the last stair as she came to an abrupt halt. Jon lay stretched on her couch, wearing the clothes he'd been in last night. He used a cushion under his head for a pillow. Without a blanket he must have spent a chilly night, but it seemed not to have kept him from sleeping soundly.

All her anger and frustration boiled over into a seething temper. She marched around the end of the couch and jabbed him in the shoulder. "What are you doing here?"

"Huh?" His eyes blinked open, and he squinted against the morning sun streaming through the eastern windows.

"I said, what are you doing here?" She accompanied the question with another jab, this time at his chest.

He grew more alert. "I *was* sleeping. Stop poking me."

"I'll poke you if I want. You're in my house and on my couch without permission. You're trespassing. I think I'll call a cop. Wait, you're a cop. You should arrest yourself."

"Ha."

She didn't like the gleam in his eyes. "Maybe I'll call nine-one-one and see if they'll send out a squad car. Let you explain yourself to a couple of uniforms."

When she reached across him to grab the phone on the end table, he moved with surprising speed for having just woken. She found herself sprawled on top of six feet of warm male. Cooper let out an excited bark.

When she parted her lips in protest Jon covered them with his, tangling his fingers in her hair as he cupped her head. Off guard, she let out a low moan.

Oh God, she needed this. It was wrong, he was wrong, but the kiss the night before had sparked an insatiable hunger, one that made her crave his touch like an addict.

He kissed her with an intensity that had her heart fluttering. Heat coiled from low in her belly as his lips moved over her face. The roughness from his morning beard against the sensitive skin beneath her ear had her shuddering.

She couldn't help her reaction. He tasted too good, and it was like a drug flowing through her body, making her tingle all the way to her fingers and toes. As his mouth returned hungrily to hers, emotions she'd held bottled tightly broke loose. Her body burned for him, and she groaned in frustration, kissing him with everything she had.

He deepened the kiss, his tongue sliding against hers, the evidence of his desire pulsing hard against her as his sure hands stroked along her back where her tank had ridden up to expose bare skin.

She stifled a groan when his warm fingers slipped under the elastic of her pants to caress low along her hip. Self-preservation surfaced and she broke the kiss, angling her face away from his.

Undeterred, he pressed his mouth her neck. She gave his chest a firm push. As with any drug, too much and she'd overdose.

"Jon, stop."

"Why?" His voice was muffled as he turned his face into her hair and breathed in.

She raised her head. "Because I don't want to OD."

He lay back against the cushion to gaze at her from under heavy lids, his fingers still tangled in her hair. He looked warm and rumpled and sexy. "You want to run that one by me again?"

"You're a drug, and I don't want to OD."

"Whatever that means."

She pushed up with her arms, the contact bringing her more firmly against the hardness nestled against her thigh.

"You're killing me, Rane."

With his arms encircling her, he shifted them until they were lying on their sides, facing each other. He stroked a finger lightly along her temple.

"Don't."

He stared at her. "Are you telling me you don't feel anything for me?"

"It doesn't matter what I feel. This, what you're doing, is all an act."

He groaned. "Bullshit. You felt how much this isn't an act."

"You'd have that reaction with any woman lying on top of you."

He gave a harsh laugh. "No, sweetheart, this is all you. There's something between us. You feel it, too."

She sat up. Cooper cocked his head to one side as he watched her with avid interest, which told her he wanted his breakfast.

"I don't trust you. You lied to me. This sudden inability to keep your hands to yourself is fake. I can't help that I reacted too." She shrugged. "I'm human." To keep it from happening again she forced herself to stand on wobbly legs and moved to a chair across the room. "You won't be kissing me again."

Shifting to sit back against the cushions, he rested his feet on the edge of the coffee table. "Okay, unless you want it, too."

Figuring it wise to ignore that comment, she asked, "Why are you on my couch?"

He shrugged. "To keep you safe."

The stubble shadowing his jaw made her fingers itch to touch it again. Her skin was rasped in the best possible way where his beard had scratched her neck. She cleared her throat past a sudden obstruction. "I can take care of myself. I've been doing it for a long time."

"You sprayed that guy last night with pepper spray. That was good. But you couldn't take down two guys. I'm sticking around to even the odds if those two make a reappearance." His gaze remained direct. "You own a gun?"

She nodded. "I have two. They're secure in gun safes. Like I said, I can protect myself."

"Except when you can't access the gun safes. I'm assuming your father taught you to shoot."

She froze, heart thudding. She didn't want to talk about her dad with him. "He did," she said carefully.

He must have caught something in her expression. "A couple of the guys on the task force knew your dad. I'd met him. He worked in a different division, but one of my team members worked an undercover deal with him. He was a good cop."

Rane tried to read his face. Was he hiding something? Did he know what her dad had done? She needed to get Jon out of her house and out of her life before he found out enough to put her dad behind bars where Simon DiNardo would make good on this threat.

Her own complicity hardly mattered in the face of what could happen to her father.

"You need to tell me what DiNardo wanted."

She'd spent the night tossing and turning, trying to decide what to do, but suddenly she saw with clarity what had been clouded by emotion. Knowing it didn't stop her heart from sinking to her stomach. She had to tell him what Simon had asked her to do. The hardest part of was the realization she would have to trust Jon to figure out how to put Simon behind bars before her dad, or those close her, were harmed. The sooner the threat from the DiNardo family was gone, the sooner her father would be safe.

"Rane?"

"Okay. Fine. I'll talk to you." She saw him relax as if tension had suddenly eased from his body. "But first I need coffee." She rose and walked to the kitchen and he followed.

While she filled the coffee pot, he opened a bag of whole-grain bread. At her glance, he shrugged. "I'll buy you a whole shopping cart of groceries later, but I'm hungry now."

This certainly wasn't how she had thought her morning would go. With the smells of coffee and toasting bread pervading the kitchen, she set butter and jam on the table and sat down with her plate of toast. Jon sat across from her slathering enough butter on his toast to make her arteries quake. "Okay, tell me what's going on."

She didn't know what had happened to her anger. Or maybe she did. He'd kissed it away. Now she felt weary with resignation. She knew her mother leaving when she'd been a child had left her with deep-seated trust issues. Her relationship with Kyle had reinforced the belief that those who were closest to her would let her down. Jon's deception was really nothing to be surprised about, but right now she couldn't seem to summon the resentment she needed to help her maintain her distance.

"Simon told me you were a cop. I didn't believe him. I said you wouldn't lie to me." She smiled crookedly. "I guess I put my faith in the wrong guy."

He took the hit without flinching. When he spoke, his voice was hard. "That was all superficial, necessary for the job. You can trust me with the things that really matter."

"Like your name? Like why you're trying to get close to me?"

He scowled. "You can trust me to protect you. To keep you safe while we figure out how to stop the DiNardos." He waited a long moment. "What did Simon want?"

She took a sip of coffee, the warmth helping calm her jittery nerves. "He wants me to get close to you, to find out what your task force is planning. He wants me to tell him when and how you plan to set him up so he can be ready. He wants to take out your entire task force."

Blue eyes turned cool slate. "He wants you to betray me."

She nodded.

"What did he threaten you with to cooperate?"

"He said he'd hurt my dad, or shoot me on my way to work. He said if he wanted, he could kill my friend Lily or hurt Cooper." She was amazed her voice sounded so calm as she recited the list of destruction Simon had planned if she didn't cooperate. She unloaded everything. Except she wasn't telling Jon about Simon's threat to expose her father for his involvement in Kyle's conviction.

Jon gave a decisive nod. "We'll take you into protective custody. This may be over soon anyway if our takedown goes ahead today as planned." He paused, and she could almost see the thoughts racing behind his eyes. "Where's your dad? He can probably take care of himself, but he needs to know, and we can put a guy on him for protection if he wants. On your friend too."

She shook her head. "You can't put me into protective custody, or put a guy on Dad or Lily. It would tip your hand. He'd know I told you. The only way this will work is if I act like I'm cooperating, then pass along your plans and you can be ready for him."

He frowned, lowering a hand to pet Cooper who'd come to lean against his knee. "Yeah, you're right." He raised his gaze to hers. She didn't like the sudden gleam in his eyes. "I'll have to move in here with you. I can't protect you if I'm up in the apartment. If Simon finds out, then all the better. He'll think you're moving ahead on getting close to me."

Chapter Seven

Rane jogged to the employee entrance of St. Augustine's. Her discussion with Jon and a quick stop at her father's facility had made her late. She'd had no choice. She made arrangements to insure no one could visit her father unless she preapproved them.

During breakfast, she'd told Jon about her father's Alzheimer's diagnosis. She hadn't expected him to understand how agonizing the decision had been to put him in a facility, but Jon had gotten it. She'd been watching him carefully, and it hadn't seemed like his interest in her father was anything more than typical curiosity.

Even if her father couldn't be put on trial because of his mental state, she didn't want what he'd done public knowledge. It would vacate Kyle's conviction, and he'd be compensated by the state, which was ludicrous since he'd served less time for the drug charge than he would for the murder he'd committed.

She shut her locker, spun the dial on the lock, and hurried into the emergency room. The other nurses told her the morning had been slow, but from the time her shift started there was a steady uptick in patients. By mid-afternoon they had a two hour wait for non-emergency walk-ins.

Returning with Lily from a quick break, a flurry of activity at the entry doors drew her attention. An ambulance crew was rushing in a man strapped to a gurney. He had an oxygen mask over his nose and mouth, a bandage across his forehead, and his shirt was cut open where an EMT applied pressure to a chest wound.

Behind the EMT, a big guy held up a bag of clear fluid attached by a tube to the injured man. She rushed forward with Lily as the guy snapped out, "He's a cop. You better not let him die."

The big guy had wild blond hair and a stubbly beard. *Oh no.* He was the man who'd helped Jon move into the apartment. Heart faltering, she jogged to the gurney, desperately scanning the patient's features. The thick blondish-brown hair and high cheek bones were the same, but this man wasn't Jon.

"Rane, grab the bag," Lily ordered.

The urgency in her voice made Rane pull herself together. She donned gloves and took the saline bag from Jon's friend while the EMT briefed them on the injuries. An abrasion to the forehead and a bullet-wound to the chest. The bullet had entered under the rib cage and exited out the back. They pushed him into a curtained enclosure and began assessing his injuries.

Dr. Grayson strode in and within minutes the patient was on his way to the operating room, where'd they'd use a portable x-ray machine to detect any bullet fragments and determine how much damage had been done.

She drew back the curtain in time to see Jon charging through the double doors of the ER. His friend intercepted him, grabbing his shoulders to hold him back.

"Where the hell's Nathan? How bad is he?"

"Jon," she called out. She hurried to him.

He whirled at the sound of her voice. "Where is he? Where's my brother?"

She laid a hand on his arm. "He's on his way to surgery." When he began to pull away like he would chase down the gurney and check for himself, she tightened her hold. "Listen to me. He looks okay. The bullet was a through and through. It doesn't look like any organs were nicked. He'll have tissue damage, but the bleeding is controlled and his vitals are good."

Jon took a deep breath and let it out slowly. "Okay. Good. That's good. When can I see him?" He ran unsteady fingers through his hair.

When he raised his arm, her gaze latched onto the deep red stain on Jon's shirt visible under his jacket. "You're hurt. Come with me."

"I'm fine. I want to see my brother."

"That wasn't a request." She turned to the big blond guy. "Are you shot too?"

He shook his head. "No. ma'am. I'm good. Take care of my buds."

She held out a hand to Jon. "Come with me."

Taking her hand in a firm grip, he turned to the other man. "Ben, come get me if you hear anything." At Ben's nod, Jon let Rane lead him through a curtain to an empty bed.

Once he had his jacket off and was lying down, Rane eased up his shirt. A bullet had grazed the skin above his hip, deeply scoring his flesh, but leaving the muscle below undamaged. She didn't like to think of how close he'd come to being seriously injured.

She pulled supplies from a cabinet and began cleaning the wound, conscious of his intense gaze on her.

"Is he really okay?"

She glanced at his face. It looked like he was biting back on the pain, his blue eyes burned fierce. "He's not now, but he will be. What happened?"

Jon closed his eyes. He was flagging. Most likely from adrenaline crash.

"DiNardos wanted to keep their drugs. An informant told us about a stash house where they were holding heroin to be cut for distribution. A lot of dope in there and they didn't want to give it up. Don't know how they were expecting us. They had automatic rifles. Nasty firefight."

He sucked in a breath when she applied antiseptic. Working steadily, she packed the area with gauze and applied tape. After disposing of the packaging, she pulled off her gloves. "Okay, soldier. I think you'll live."

When he caught her hand, she shifted her gaze to his. The muscle in his jaw jumped, and his eyes flashed with fire. Too much emotion for Rane to deal with. Her stupid heart wanted to trust him, but her brain told her to be cautious.

She pulled free, and moved to the curtain.

"I'll get your paperwork."

***

Jon leaned back in an uncomfortable chair upholstered in butt-ugly green. The pain in his side throbbed like ten sore teeth. The clock on the wall said it was almost midnight. Nathan had been out of recovery and had been in this room for a couple of hours. He lay motionless in the muted light, tubes and wires hooking him up to bags. Monitors made annoying humming and beeping sounds. The doctor had assured Jon his brother would make a full recovery, but looking at him now, Jon thought Nate looked like he belonged in the morgue.

The door opened and he sat up. He recognized the nurse, a curvy woman with golden eyes. Lily. Her name was Lily, and she was a friend of Rane's. She carried a tablet, but instead of going directly to the monitors, as he'd seen the other nurse do, Lily stopped by Nathan's bed to study her patient.

"Hey."

She glanced over at him. "Hey back. You don't look so comfortable on that chair, detective."

"I can't leave. He's my brother. I have to be sure he's okay." He frowned. "Aren't you an ER nurse?"

She shrugged. "Sometimes I like to check up on my patients to see how they're doing." She turned to the monitors. "Everything's looking good. He's a pretty tough guy to come through getting shot as well as he did."

Jon found himself swallowing past a lump in his throat. "Yeah. He's a tough guy, all right. I'm glad you think he looks good 'cause he looks like hell to me." He rose to stand beside the bed, his hands shoved into his pockets.

The door opened again and Rane walked in. Her gaze found his, and she crossed to stand beside Lily. She looked at Nathan, then glanced at the monitors before looking back at Jon. "He looks good."

"That's what people keep telling me."

"They're right. You should go. Get some sleep."

"When are you off shift?" He could see the weariness around her eyes.

"Now."

"Hey there, cowboy," Lily spoke quietly.

Nathan had his eyes open and focused on Lily as she bent over him.

"You're beautiful." His voice sounded raspy.

Lily gave a soft laugh. "Well, you sure woke up fine."

"Really, you're beautiful."

She smiled at him. "Those are some good drugs they've got you on, big guy. Make you a little loopy. You probably won't remember this conversation in the morning."

"Nate." Jon felt relief flood through him when his brother turned his head to him. He'd been shot, he'd been through surgery, but he was there alive, aware of the world around him.

"JonJon. What the hell happened?"

"They knew we were coming, that's what the hell happened. We were outgunned."

Nathan tried to raise a hand but he was hung up by tubes. "Shit."

"Detective Garretson, your brother needs to rest."

Jon glanced at Lily. It was then he noticed Rane had left. He gave Lily a curt nod. His brother had been through hell. Their talk could wait until morning.

"Now that I can see you're not dead, I'm going home."

At his brother's nod, Jon gave him a half smile. "I'll leave you in beautiful Lily's capable hands."

***

Jon leaned back against the wall near the employee entrance. The temperature had dropped and a steady rain fell from low clouds. He felt drained. Completely and utterly drained. Part of it was post-adrenaline crash. There'd been that initial surge of alarm when the task force had come under fire. They'd taken cover, returned fire, and fought like hell until gaining the upper hand. Then the mind-numbing fear when he'd realized Nathan had been hit. Follow that with hours of waiting and Jon's brain was numb. His brother was good, he would come through this with a battle scar, but with all his important parts intact.

Jon hunched his shoulders when a gust of wind drove rain under the eaves. The door opened and he glanced over. A doctor in a long white coat. He wondered why they wore white coats. Why not blue? Or green? Jon turned up his collar and waited, trying to ignore the gnawing ache on his side where the bullet had grazed him. Hardly serious, but it burned. The door opened again and this time he straightened.

"Rane."

She had a small backpack slung over her shoulder, her hospital credentials dangled from her fingers on a lanyard, and her beautiful long hair was hidden under a knit beanie.

She stopped at his voice and he saw her hesitation. When she turned, wariness lined her expression. "What do you want?"

He almost slipped and said *you*. He fought the urge to put his arms around her, to hold her and be held. Not the right time or place. "A ride home?"

"Where's your truck?"

"At the station. I came here in a squad car."

She paused before finally saying, "Okay."

He wasn't sure how to read her. She seemed subdued, closed off.

That morning she'd been upset, but after they'd talked, he thought she'd understood his motivations. He watched her carefully. He could have sworn that between the time he'd seen her in Nathan's room and now, her burden had doubled. Uneasy, he moved to her side, casting his gaze around the parking lot, looking for anyone out of place.

"Anything going on?"

She didn't answer. She tugged down her beanie and stepped into the rain.

They walked across the wet pavement to her car.

"Rane."

She shook her head, the car locks disengaging when she reached for the door handle. Feeling edgy, Jon opened the passenger door and slid into the seat and out of the rain.

Before she pressed the start button, he grabbed her hand. He rubbed his thumb across her knuckles and waited until she turned to face him. After a long look, she tugged her hand free and reached into her coat pocket. She pulled out a folded slip of paper and silently handed it to him.

He unfolded it, the letters on the paper barely visible in the dim light. He squinted and read. "'Mr. Bojangles'? Where'd this come from?"

"It was in my locker. Someone slipped it in through the louvers when I was on shift."

He stared at the note. "Why Mr. Bojangles? Does it mean anything to you?"

"It's a song from the seventies. My dad's had it stuck in his head for the past week. He's been singing it over and over."

Jon frowned. "It's got to be from DiNardo. It means he's seen your dad. The bastard has been to see your dad again and sent you a warning."

She started the car and backed out of the parking space. "I don't know if he saw him again. I went to dad's facility this morning to make sure only people I've approved can visit him. Could be one of the nurses is reporting to Simon. I think someone on the staff might be one of his people."

Jon watched the streetlights reflected off the wet pavement as they sped down the road. Rain pattered against the windshield, and one of the wiper blades trailed a piece of rubber back and forth across the glass. "Why do you think that?"

"Something Simon said last night about the nurses. I've wondered if he might have sources inside hospital or senior homes like my dad's where they could get their hands on Oxy. These kids aren't starting with heroin. They're getting hooked on other stuff first then graduating to heroin."

"You're right about that. We've been working that angle."

They drove through the dark streets until they reached her driveway. Getting out of the car, they walked to the house as a fitful wind blew the rain down in fat drops.

At the kitchen door she paused, jingling her keys in her hand, her expression uncertain. Cooper whined on the other side of the door. They stood under the outside light and he raised a brow at her hesitation. "Rane, you're under my protection. I'm coming in. I'm not letting you stay by yourself tonight. You need to get used to that reality."

She frowned. "You didn't need a ride tonight, did you? You've been assigned to stick to me because of Simon."

He laughed. "I really did need a ride. Can we go in? Cooper wants his dinner." She gave him the classic pissed-off-woman eye roll. She unlocked the door and stepped inside, going down on one knee to greet her dog with a body rub as Jon followed her in.

***

Rane did her best to ignore Jon. She fed Cooper and went upstairs. When she came back down, dressed in stretchy pants and a loose sweatshirt, she found the man leaning against the kitchen counter, a beer in hand. He still wore the shirt stained with his blood. He tipped the bottle toward her. "Want some?"

She eyed him warily. "Where'd you get that?"

His expression remained neutral. "Fridge."

Uncertain, she turned to open the refrigerator door. When she'd made her breakfast that morning the shelves had been barely half full. Now they were brimming with more food than she could eat in a week. It wasn't hard to figure out who was responsible.

Bottles of Jon's favorite micro-brewery beer lined the door and little tubs of her brand of Greek yogurt were stacked on a shelf. Shaking her head, she reached for the English muffins and peanut butter. Holding them up, she raised her brows in question.

He shook his head. Instead, he turned to open a cupboard and pulled down a box of cereal, not a brand she usually bought.

"Thank you."

He shot her a questioning look.

"For the groceries. You don't have to, you know. I never cared about you eating my food."

"I do. I know you don't want me here, and I'm sorry about that. The least I can do is help out with the groceries."

She nodded. She didn't want him in her house for several reasons. The top of the list should've been the risk he'd figure out her dad's involvement in Kyle's conviction. But right now, struggling against this crazy attraction when he was assigned to stay close felt equally dangerous.

Beyond that, she had to admit the note in her locker had rattled her, and Jon made her feel safe. He set his cereal and beer on the table and went to the door to the backyard to let Cooper in. "You have a towel to dry his feet?"

"I'll do it." She walked to the cupboard by the door and pulled out an ancient towel. When she turned Jon held out a hand.

"I'll take care of it."

"No, thanks. He's my dog."

"Rane." He ran his hand down the ends of her hair, his expression patient. "Don't do this. You're trying to keep me out, to keep me at a distance. I'm in this with you."

"No. You can't touch me." The words came out sharp and defensive. She didn't care. Her self-preservation was on the line here. She backed away. "I get that you have to be here. Here with me in the house. It's part of your assignment. But I won't go along with it if it means physical contact. I can't deal with that."

He lifted his hands, backing away, his blue eyes sharp. "You know this is more than an assignment to me. *You're* more than an assignment to me."

She shrugged. "Maybe. It doesn't matter. I don't want you to touch me."

"Fine." He pulled the towel out of her hand. "But I'm taking care of the damn dog." When he was done, he strode out the kitchen door, and she could hear him pounding up the stairs to his apartment. He came back a few minutes later with some clothes and a few toiletries. Knowing she didn't really have any choice in the matter, she didn't say a word.

It was nearly one in the morning by the time Rane showed Jon the guest bedroom. She'd seriously considered letting him continue sleeping on the couch. The funny thing was, she knew he'd have done it without argument. Maybe that was why she found herself turning on the light in the bedroom next to hers. Before she could go to bed and escape into the oblivion of sleep, though, conscience dictated she had one more thing to do.

She stopped Jon when he would've walked past her into the room. "I need to check your bandages. The bathroom's over here."

She led the way across the hall. When she realized he hadn't followed she turned and looked at him expectantly.

"I'm fine."

"Right. You've been shot, but you're fine. Come here."

"No. I'll look after it myself. I know how to change a bandage."

She blew out a gusty breath. "Would you stop arguing and get in here?"

He tipped his head back, staring at the ceiling as if searching for salvation before looking back at her with an expression that seemed desperate.

"Problem?"

He shook his head. "What could be the problem? Let's get the damned thing taken care of."

She frowned as he brushed past her going into the bathroom. "Okay. It'll be easier if you take off your shirt. It's a mess anyway."

Glancing in the mirror, she caught his reluctant expression as he started on the buttons. Puzzled, she opened the medicine cabinet and pulled out packages of gauze, swabs, tape, and a bottle of betadine.

"Really, no need to be shy." Turning to face him she about swallowed her tongue. That morning she'd been focused on his wound. Now? Wow. Golden chest hair highlighted well-defined pecs, and rippling abs made her mouth water. Then there were the strong trapezius muscles sloping to powerful deltoids. The man had amazing shoulders and she'd always been a sucker for good shoulders. Altogether, he'd have been the perfect model for the human anatomy classes she'd taken in college.

With his head bent, Jon tugged on a corner of the tape. He looked up suddenly and Rane hoped she'd hidden her reaction.

"Umm, you'd better sit on the counter. The light is best there."

"Sure." In jeans slung low across his hips he pushed himself onto the counter. His wince helped her to focus on something other than the play of muscle across his chest. She tugged off the tape and then the gauze to reveal the wound below. "Have you taken the pain meds I gave you?"

"No."

She glanced up at him. "Why not? I can tell this is sore."

"I just didn't."

She gave him a searching look before turning back to the wound. "It's looking good. The color is as it should be, and it's beginning to heal." She applied a fresh pad and then a bandage, smoothing it against warm skin. "I want you to take those meds. The added benefit is they'll make you drowsy and help you sleep. Where are they?"

"I left them in my jacket downstairs. I'm not taking them."

She straightened, her hand still pressed against the bandage at his waist. She became aware that she was standing between his legs and his gaze was intense.

"I knew this was a bad idea."

She could agree, but wouldn't say so.

"Why won't you take the meds? You need the rest and you don't want to be in pain."

He gave her a hard look, then surprised her by taking her hand from his waist and turning it so he could press a warm kiss into her palm. "Sweetheart, you're testing my resolve here. Now stand back."

"But—"

Letting go of her hand, he cupped her shoulders and moved her back before sliding off the counter. He reached for his shirt.

"Jon."

"Look, if I took the pain meds and zonked out, I wouldn't be much help if you were in danger. You have Tylenol?" She nodded. "I'll take a couple Tylenol."

Rane took a bottle from the medicine cabinet. She shook out two tablets and dropped them into his open palm. Before she could reach for the little paper cups on the shelf, he tossed the pills into his mouth and ducked his head to the faucet. Turning it on, he splashed water on his face then took a mouthful to swallow down the pills. He dried his face on a towel, hung it carefully, and then leaned down to give her a swift kiss on the lips. He smiled at her crookedly. "Sorry. Couldn't help myself. Thanks for the TLC. Good night, sweetheart."

Chapter Eight

"How do we know we can trust her? Did you tell her about the hit yesterday? She could be playing both sides."

"What the hell, McCray? She's a nurse at St. Augie's. Her father was a goddamn cop." Jon scowled. "You wouldn't recognize integrity if it hit you on the head."

"Then how did the DiNardos know about the stash house yesterday? You let something slip when you were cozied up at her place?" McCray huffed. "I don't trust her."

Rane wondered if the guy was contrary by nature or if he just liked messing with people. Jon looked like he'd get a lot of satisfaction from throwing him across the room. "Aah, gentlemen? I'm sitting right here. Why don't you ask me your questions?" Heads swiveled toward her.

"All right then, why don't we start with your relationship with Kyle DiNardo?" Ty McCray frowned at her, his expression filled with distrust. "It's suspicious as fuck that you two were hooked up and the minute you drop him he ends up convicted for possession with intent. You want us to believe you didn't know he was dealing all the time you were together? Maybe you were okay with it. Maybe you made a little money on the side selling to the other little coeds."

The guy was being a jerk but Rane thought she should cut him some slack. It was obvious the entire team had been shaken by the ambush, and by Nathan being shot. They were a hard, rugged group of men. All four looked like brawlers who got in street fights for fun. One of their own being injured had to be an unwelcome reminder of their mortality.

"Easy, Ty." This came from Denton, the senior detective in charge of the task force, a tall Black man built like a wall who Rane liked immediately. He'd asked about Nathan first, and then gave Jon an encouraging back slap that would have sent most men to their knees.

She glanced at Jon. He had a fist clenched and looked about ready to start pounding on something, probably Ty.

Taking a deep breath, she spoke up. "Kyle and I were both pretty young when we were dating. He was idealistic. He knew what his family was into and thought he could break the cycle. He wanted to go to college to be a forest ranger. Simon wouldn't allow it."

She scanned the room. All eyes were on her, some more friendly than others. Jon still didn't look happy, but he wasn't interrupting.

"What do you mean, he wouldn't allow it?" Ben asked, his wild hair confined beneath a Sounders beanie.

"Simon has certain expectations about what family means and does. Family doesn't turn its back on family."

"Sounds like big brother wouldn't have liked you too much, seeing as how your old man was a cop," Ben commented, voice gravelly. Like the rest of the task force, he didn't appear to have gotten much sleep.

Rane nodded. As always her stomach knotted when anyone mentioned her father. "He didn't. Simon keeps an iron grip on that family, but I think Kyle could be his weakness. Their father died when Kyle was ten or eleven, and I think Simon took on that role. In some ways, I think he was letting Kyle be a kid before having to face the reality of the family business. Regardless, he made it pretty clear there was no other option but the family business." She shrugged. "I guess it backfired on him."

"So you're saying Kyle didn't want to be part of the drug business. What changed?" Jon asked. Fatigue lined his face. The Tylenol wouldn't have been enough to alleviate the pain from the bullet wound, and with the added worry over Nathan, Jon had probably had little or no sleep. She'd gone with him to St. Augustine's that morning to check on Nathan and found he was running a slight fever. Assurances that he would get better hadn't eased Jon's concern.

Returning her attention to the conversation, Rane continued. "I can't pinpoint anything in particular. I wasn't around. I'd gone away to college. When I came back for the holidays, Kyle was different. It was like a light had gone out in him. I broke up with him after he'd gotten in a fight with some guy when we'd gone out for the evening. It was about the time I realized he'd started dealing."

"When was this?"

Rane thought back. "Probably six years ago." She saw something flicker in Jon's eyes, and his expression hardened. She wondered what could have happened six years ago to bring that reaction.

"We need to give her something." When all eyes turned to Jon he continued. "We've got to give her something she can pass onto Simon. We need to take a look at the staff at St. Augustine's and at Doug Smith's facility. Simon is stepping up his game, and that means we have to step up ours."

"We're not giving that bastard shit." This came from McCray.

"Jon's right," Denton's voice held the easy authority of leadership. "DiNardo's got to believe she's still on board with his plan. She could tell him we know about the other stash house, the one on South Dearborn. That we're getting ready to move on it."

"No way." Ty turned to Denton, his face red under his grizzled beard. "I've worked undercover in that neighborhood for the last month. I want to arrest those bastards, not let them skate out of there."

Denton held up a calming hand. "Think about it, Ty. We're after bigger fish than petty dealers. We'll get them eventually, but we need to play this right to get the DiNardos."

The conversation went back and forth for several minutes. Jon stayed quiet, letting Denton convince the others. In the end, McCray was still unhappy, but was in agreement that she was to give Simon the tip.

She hoped it would be enough to satisfy him.

***

Rane leaned back on the slippery vinyl couch in the ER staff lounge while sipping lukewarm tea. She eyed Lily speculatively. Her friend had been jittery all afternoon. "Okay, spill. You look like you're about to pop."

"Trust you to notice." Lily sat forward on the padded ottoman, tapping her fingers on her knees. "Okay, okay. I'll tell you, but you can't tell anyone."

"Right. No blabbing. Now shoot."

"Dr. G asked me out."

"He did? When did this happen?"

"When I came on shift today. He stopped me in the parking lot. Asked if I wanted to go to dinner with him. Maybe catch a movie."

"Hot damn. When's the big night? We need to get you some sexy underwear."

"Really? You think I'll have sex with him on the first date?"

"Of course not." Rane grinned. "You'll feel sexier knowing you're wearing hot underwear. He'll get the vibes and it'll drive him crazy because he'll *know* there's no way he'll get to see your underwear, being the first date and all."

"You're really devious, you know that, right?" Lily's eyes glowed.

"Yep. So when's the date?"

"It's not."

"What? What do you mean it's not? You said yes, didn't you?"

"Nope."

Rane narrowed her eyes, studying her friend for signs of insanity. "Lily. You've been mooning over the guy like you wanted him to ask you to prom for a month now. He asks and you say no? You're not well."

"Maybe I've gotten over him."

Leaning forward, Rane put a cool hand to her friend's forehead. "You don't have a fever. Maybe we can get you in for an MRI, look for brain trauma."

"No brain trauma, but maybe something is wrong with me. Some other guy catches my eye and it's like Sam Grayson doesn't exist."

Rane put her hands to her head, thinking it might spin off her shoulders. "What other guy? There's no other guy."

"There is. You met him."

"Who?"

"You'll think I'm nuts."

"Who, Lily?"

"Nathan Garretson."

Rane let that sink in, then let out a low laugh. "Well, then we're both nuts. If he's anything like his brother, I understand perfectly."

***

Shutting her locker at the end of her shift, Rane felt her phone vibrating in her pocket. She glanced at the text.

Wait for me. Running late.

She rolled her eyes. She should have taken her car but Jon insisted on driving her to the hospital every day. She knew he had better things to do, but he was adamant. Or more aptly, stubborn. People at work were commenting on her new "boyfriend," which, she guessed, was the point. Mostly.

While Jon had insisted it was for her safety, she knew the task force had been digging and had identified someone at St. Augustine's they thought could be responsible for the Oxy stolen from the hospital pharmacy turning up on the streets. Leaving the plant in place meant the person might see her riding back and forth with Jon. Getting closer to the cop just as Simon had ordered.

Needing fresh air, she exited the employee entrance and headed to a picnic area next to the parking lot. Stars shone brilliantly in the night sky while a chilly gust of wind let her know fall had definitely arrived. She tugged her beanie more snugly around her ears. She sat on a bench and pulled her coat tight around her and leaned back against the table. She took out her phone to check her email. From the corner of her eye she saw a figure approach. Expecting Jon, she glanced up.

Her mind blanked for a long moment. "Kyle."

"Rane."

He appeared gaunt and pale, as if prison had left a dirty residue that couldn't be scrubbed off. Hands thrust deeply in the pockets of a navy pea coat, he stood looking at her, expression inscrutable. "You look good."

"Thanks." She didn't know what to make of him. She'd feared this moment for so long, but he didn't look threatening. More at a loss for what to say. "What are you doing here?"

"I need to talk to you."

"Kyle, I don't think that's a good idea."

He shook his head. "You're in danger, Rane. I know your boyfriend will be here to get you soon, so we can't talk now." He paused to scan the street that ran next to the employee parking lot. He turned his gaze back to her, his shadowed eyes unfathomable. "Will you meet me on your lunchbreak? Not tomorrow, but the day after?"

"Where?"

"Right here." The half-smile he gave her held an echo of the engaging young man he used to be. "I can sit with you while you're eating your lunch."

"Okay." She didn't know why she agreed, but she felt he had something important to tell her.

He nodded toward the street. "There's your ride."

Rane looked out to see Jon's black truck pulling into the lot. By the time she turned back Kyle was gone, melting into the shifting shadows of the windy night.

Hurrying to the truck, Rane opened the door and was met with a blast of classic Pearl Jam. Jon turned down the volume and leaned back in his seat as he waited for her to buckle in. Snapping the belt in place, she pulled off her beanie. "Hey."

When the truck didn't move she glanced at him. He sat watching her with a focused intensity she felt like a physical touch. Like he really *saw* her—saw beneath the surface to what really mattered.

He reached across the cab to cup a hand to the back of her neck and pull her toward him. His lips met hers in a kiss made all the more seductive because he hadn't said a word. She felt herself drawn in, sighing in pleasure when his warm fingers threaded into her hair. A deep curl of need rose from deep in her belly and had her fighting back a response. She'd tried to put the brakes on her attraction but wondered if, like her, he'd reached his limit.

Living in the same house, being in close proximity day after day, had certainly put her on the edge. His heart beat heavily under the palm she'd pressed against his chest. A car horn blared behind them.

He took his time breaking the kiss, finally releasing her to sit back and ease his foot off the brake.

"Wow."

He glanced at her. In the faint light from the dashboard she could see his eyes glitter with amusement. He stopped to check for traffic before pulling into the street. "Wow?"

"Yeah, wow. You're really good at that."

"I'd like to think it's that we're good at it together."

They were, and that was beginning to worry her. He drove through the alternating light and dark that was the city streets at night while she pondered the changing tone of their relationship.

"How was your shift?"

"Huh?"

"Your shift, Rane. At the hospital."

"Yeah, my shift." She could see him grinning and made an effort to get her brain cells in order. "The shift was fine." She paused, suddenly remembering what his kiss had blown out of her mind. "Kyle came by."

"To the hospital? What did he want?" She felt the instant shift in Jon's mood to high alert.

"He approached me when I went outside to wait for you. He wants to talk."

Jon's hand tightened on the steering wheel. "Why the hell didn't you stay inside? I would've texted when I got there."

"Because I wanted some fresh air. Jon, he isn't a threat. As much as I was worried that he might want to hurt me, I was wrong. I'm meeting him at the picnic tables on my lunchbreak the day after tomorrow." She frowned, something about what Kyle had said bothered her, but she couldn't put her finger on it.

Jon pulled into her driveway and brought the truck to an abrupt halt in front of the garage. He drummed his fingers on the steering wheel. "Okay. I don't like it, but we'll have a couple of guys on you."

She pushed open the door and turned to slide out of the truck, a gust of wind pulling at her hair. "You don't need to have guys on us. I'll tell you what he says."

He got out and continued his thought. "No, I don't want to leave anything to chance. We'll have our guys dressed like they're on the hospital maintenance crew. They can sit on the benches, eat lunch. Keep an eye out."

She circled the hood to where he was standing, frustration growing. "Jeez. It's not like he's going to pull out a gun and shoot me right there. For real, he didn't seem threatening."

He reached out to grasp the front of her coat, pulling her up until they were nose to nose, his eyes boring into hers. "You don't get it, do you?"

"Get what?" She swatted at his hands. "Let me go."

He released her as suddenly as he'd grabbed her. "Go inside. I need a minute." He turned and stalked down the driveway.

Fuming, Rane pulled her keys from her purse. She found the right one and jammed it into to lock. Cooper's exuberant greeting served to cool her anger. She hung her keys on the hook, let the dog into the backyard, all the while going over the scene with Jon. What had just happened?

After mixing kibble and canned food she put Cooper's dish outside and brought in his water bowl to refill.

Okay, she understood Jon wanted to keep her safe, she got that. But she really believed Simon was the threat, not Kyle. His demeanor when he'd approached her had calmed some of her anxiety about him. She needed to feed the DiNardos the information on the stash house to keep Simon satisfied, and she'd rather do that talking to Kyle than to Simon. He was psychotic.

Going through her chores, she kept an ear out for Jon. She let the dog in, loaded the dishwasher, straightened a few things, and when Jon still hadn't returned she gave up and headed upstairs. In flannel pants and a t-shirt she stood at the bathroom sink brushing her teeth when, finally, the sound of the kitchen door opening reached her.

Deciding she didn't need to figure him out at that moment, she rinsed, dried her hands, and walked into her bedroom.

"Rane."

She paused, his form a dark shadow in the hall. "What?"

"I'm sorry."

She crossed the room to lean against the doorjamb, arms folded in front of her. "Really? For what?"

"For overreacting."

She shrugged. "I get you think Kyle is dangerous, but we'll be in the open, and there'll be plenty of people around. I wouldn't meet with him if I thought he was a threat."

"I don't think I overreacted to Kyle approaching you. It's the other thing."

"Other thing?"

"That you don't believe I'm attracted to you. When I tell you this isn't just a job to me, that *you're* not just a job to me, I'm not bullshitting you."

She swallowed past her tight throat. "Maybe I believe you. Kind of."

"Kind of? You know what I think? I think you have trouble trusting people. You have trouble trusting me."

"Yeah, because you lied to me."

"We're past that, and you know it. You won't let yourself trust my feelings for you. Or yours for me."

"Who says I have feelings for you?"

"I do. They're there every time I kiss you. You can't hide from me."

Rane was silent for a long moment. "Okay."

"Okay what?"

"Okay, you're right. I *know* I have trust issues."

"Want me to guess why?"

She eyed him warily. "I already know why."

"Your mother?"

Rane stood still.

"I'm right, aren't I?"

"It's not so hard to guess, even if you are a detective. I don't have family except for my dad. Obviously, something must've happened to my mother."

"You'd said she'd left when you were a kid. I'm guessing she and your dad divorced?"

"Eventually. When I was ten, I came home from school and she'd gone. She'd packed all her clothes, but left everything else. She walked away from us."

"What'd you do?"

"What could I do? Dad said she'd met someone else. They'd been having trouble for a while. They'd have arguments. I would wake up at night and hear them yelling at each other."

"She didn't only leave your dad. She left you too."

"Yeah. It sucked. I was mad for a long time. Until finally I realized Dad hadn't left, and that he was trying really hard to be a good father."

"Was he a good father?"

"Yeah. He's the best."

"Now he's left you, too."

She tilted her head. "Huh? My dad hasn't left me."

Jon moved closer, reaching out to tug on the ends of her hair, his face shadowed. "He has. Not intentionally. Little by little his mind's going, and he's leaving you."

Rane crossed her arms in front of her. "So, what? Now you're a shrink?"

"No. I pay attention to the people I care about. When I pay attention I can usually figure out what's going on in their heads." His hand cupped her neck, thumb stroking under her ear.

"We've got to stop this."

"See? That's you not trusting me."

"Bullshit. That's me not wanting to get involved."

"Too late. We're already involved. Every time we move a little closer you want to push me away because you don't trust me."

"Can you blame me? You started off lying to me."

"We've gone over this. It's behind us."

He leaned forward, stopping so close she could feel his breath on her lips.

Then he backed away, leaving her with a gnawing ache inside. "One of these days, you'll kiss me first." His steady gaze held hers. "Go out with me."

"Like on a date?"

"Yeah. On a date. I want to get to know you outside of the case. Let's go out tomorrow night."

She eyed him speculatively. "Casual or dressed up?"

"Dressed up. Definitely dressed up."

***

"So now you're the one with the hot date. Do *you* have sexy underwear?"

"Probably. Somewhere. You're looking smug." Rane pulled a tablet toward her, checked her watch, and typed a note.

Lily laughed. "I'm feeling smug."

They were taking a minute and sitting at the nurses' station, grateful for the relatively calm afternoon.

"Where is he taking you?" Lily sat back in her chair, stretching.

"I don't know. He'd only say he needed to work out the details and to be ready by seven."

"Sounds mysterious."

"We'll see." Rane thought she had never seen her friend look so alive. "Soooo, what's going on with you and the other Garretson brother?"

"He's been released."

"Good to hear, but that doesn't answer the question."

"He asked me to come home with him and be his nurse."

"Yeah? He wants a little personal TLC?"

"I don't think that little fantasy is happening, but he did ask for my phone number." Uncertainty clouded her face.

"Did you give it to him?"

"Yeah. But I don't know if that's how he operates. If he flirts with all the women or if he really likes me."

Rane gave that some thought. "I guess you'll find out. If he's anything like his brother, I'd say he really likes you."

Lily gave Rane one of her direct looks. "Explain."

Rane shrugged, suddenly uncomfortable. "I don't know. Jon's up front with his emotions. He doesn't equivocate. He's let me know what he's feeling." She hadn't told Lily Jon had been undercover when he'd originally rented the apartment. All her friend knew was that Rane had rented to a cop and they'd gotten close.

Despite what she'd said to him, she knew she could trust him with her life.

A monitor sounded and Lily rose. "We'll have to talk about this again. I really want to know what's going on between you and Detective Cutie."

Chapter Nine

Rane fastened her seatbelt. "Where are we going?"

"Out. You look amazing."

The headlights reflected off the rain-drenched streets. Jon drove carefully, leaving a buffer between them and the car ahead. "Thank you, but you didn't answer the question."

"Don't you like surprises?"

"I hate surprises."

He glanced at her, his blue eyes gleaming, but he didn't reply to her comment.

They drove through the city until he slowed and turned into a parking lot. Rain drummed steadily on the roof, and Rane peered through the windshield. The marquis lit the night sky. "A mystery dinner playhouse?"

"Yeah. You'll like it. Sit tight for a second." Jon exited the truck and rounded the front. He opened her door holding an open umbrella. "Let's get inside before we're soaked."

They passed through ornate double doors to the lobby. Mirrors lined the walls reflecting an elaborate art deco interior and painted ceiling. Astounded, Rane spun around to take it all in.

The glamour of the Roaring Twenties was showcased in the opulent decor from the patterned carpet to the richly upholstered furniture. Staff wore boldly patterned suits and drop-waisted dresses. She felt like Scott Fitzgerald or Bessie Smith would walk by at any moment.

Rane and Jon handed their coats and umbrella to a coat check girl who smiled cheekily, her hair done like Clara Bow.

Jon's gaze traveled the length of Rane's deep burgundy sheath and stiletto heels. The fire in his eyes said her outfit had the impact she'd hoped for.

Holding her hand, Jon led her to the bar set up like a Prohibition-era speakeasy. A good number of patrons had dressed for the full experience. A woman with short-cropped curls and a flapper dress sat on a stool next to a man in a double-breasted suit coat, his fedora cocked rakishly to one side.

"This is great. Let's get cocktails, something from the twenties."

Jon nodded and motioned to the bartender who suggested a white lady. Rane went with it while Jon ordered a bourbon, neat.

"That's boring."

He grinned. "Pretend it's moonshine."

She leaned back against the bar to better watch the crowd while she sampled her drink. "This place is incredible. I've heard of it but have never been here."

He sipped his bourbon. She couldn't help noticing that while he appeared aware of the crowd, his electric gaze never strayed far from her. It'd been a long time since a man had made her feel so desirable.

"I've come a couple times. It's a lot of fun. The food's amazing and the cast is really good at getting the audience to participate in solving the mystery."

"Jon." A rail thin young man wearing black rimmed glasses and a tuxedo approached. He grinned broadly and pumped Jon's hand. "It's good to see you, man."

"You too, Rex. Looks like business has picked up." He turned to Rane. "Rane, this is Rex Gerardo, a friend of mine."

Rex's grin widened as he took Rane's hand. "Wow. You're really pretty. It's great to meet you." He motioned to the bartender. "Put their drinks on my tab. All night. You two are my guests this evening."

"Hang on. We came for an evening out, not to freeload."

Rex turned to Rane. "This guy tell you anything about me?"

She shook her head, curious. There was something between them that seemed...powerful.

"I'll tell you, then. He saved my life."

"Not true. You saved your own life. My role was to add a little extra support."

Rex shook his head, and his tone allowed for no argument. "He saved my life. I'd be dead or in prison if he hadn't seen something in me. He got me off the streets, kept tabs on me. Enrolled me in a drama program at the community center." His gaze shifted back to Jon. "The man who saved my life isn't paying for an evening out with his lady when he comes to my place." Rex's grin flashed again when Jon shifted uncomfortably. Rex said to Rane, "He introduced me to the owner, now I'm manager and love it. Your evening is on me."

Rex seated them at a table lighted by a small, ornate slag glass lamp and wished them an enjoyable evening. Rane tried to relax, to focus on the event, but even when the show began she was keenly aware Jon's attention remained focused on her. Their meal was delivered and she enjoyed the play, but her gaze kept returning to the man sitting across from her. Every time they locked gazes she felt a current spark between them.

She took a bite of her asparagus. He'd been right about the food, it was delicious. The dinner theater was fun, but she was glad the cast left them alone, prompting other guests to solve the mystery. She'd need to focus on the show to participate and being with Jon was too distracting. He'd worn a navy sport coat over a pearl-gray shirt, and a deep burgundy tie. Nothing out of the ordinary, but on him it accentuated his broad shoulders and deep chest. He looked yummy. The knowing look on his face told her he knew exactly how he affected her.

Determined to get through the evening without jumping him, she said, "Tell me, why did Rex's life need saving."

He chewed his food slowly, and she found herself watching the long column of his throat as he swallowed.

"You hear it every day. Single mom works two jobs to support her kid, but she's never home so the kid didn't have enough supervision. He started running the streets."

"How did you first meet him?"

"I grabbed him by the seat of his pants to keep him from falling off a bridge and onto a busy freeway."

"Really? So you literally saved his life. What was he doing on the bridge?"

"Tagging. The bugger tried to talk his way out of it. He fed me this elaborate story to try to explain away the backpack full of spray cans and fresh paint on the bridge. Had to give him credit for imagination."

"You saw his creativity and hooked him up with a drama program."

He shrugged, wide shoulders moving under his coat. "His mom asked for help so I started keeping tabs. Went to a couple of his performances. I guess he needed to know someone cared."

"He's lucky you did. Then you got him the position at the playhouse."

He shook his head. "He did that himself. The owner saw Rex is an original, and a quick learner. Being a smart man, he offered him the manager position. All I did was make an introduction."

"That's more than a lot of people would do."

He picked up his coffee, his long fingers wrapped around the cup. Even his hands were gorgeous. Strong. Long fingered. He stilled, eyes burning over the brim of his cup.

The electric current between them buzzed and snapped. "You keep looking at me like that and we won't make it through dinner."

"Ignore me, I'll get over it."

"I sure as hell hope you don't."

She laughed nervously. If he only knew.

It seemed like all the reasons she had for staying away from him were eroding away like sand dunes against a high tide.

Her dad was still an issue, and Jon was in danger. The DiNardos didn't have a problem firing machine guns at cops.

A real relationship would never work because she didn't do real relationships. But despite all that she really, really wanted to feel those hands on her.

She smiled grimly and stabbed a piece of chicken with her fork.

***

Rane leaned back in the truck's passenger seat. The rain had turned to mist, which was cleared by the occasional swish of the wipers. "I had a wonderful time. You get high marks for an original and fun first date."

"That all I get high marks for?"

She eyed him as he skillfully maneuvered the big truck. "You fishing for complements?"

"Trying to figure out where I stand."

The occasional streetlight illuminated Jon's strong profile. He glanced at her, then back at the road, the tension between them humming like a high voltage wire. She felt like the slightest spark could set them off.

She knew he was attracted to her, but she didn't think it bordered on addiction, which she had for him. Her resolve not to give in had pretty much dissolved, which meant she'd have to push him away for good, or go with it. There were no half-measures here.

Rane was chewing her lip when they reached the house and parked. They hustled across the driveway to get out of the cold, damp air. She opened the kitchen door and immediately Cooper was whining to be let out.

"I'll take care of this guy if you want to go upstairs."

Rane eyed Jon, but said nothing. He went through the small mudroom to let out Cooper. Instead of going for safe and no-risk upstairs, she kicked off her heels and waited for Jon. He returned to the kitchen, stopping dead in his tracks when he found her still standing in the middle of the room.

"No."

He raised a brow. "No what?"

"No, I'm not going upstairs."

"You'd be a lot safer if you did." His words were a warning reinforced by the raw hunger pulsing in his expression.

"Maybe I don't want safe."

She stepped to him, heart thudding against her ribs, and placed her hands on his chest. She went up on tiptoes to press her lips to his.

A spark caught between them, igniting a conflagration. His fingers gripped her hips, and once again she found herself backed against the kitchen wall, their mouths clashing, his tongue mating with hers. He tasted of bourbon and sin. His hands moved up her sides and brushed the underside of her breasts as his mouth continued to consume her. When he pressed his body to hers, she moaned her pleasure into his mouth.

By now she should be used to how wild with want he made her, but each kiss, each touch was a new, exotic sensation. Savoring the feel of his strong muscles shifting under her fingers, she deepened the kiss, wanting more. Wanting everything.

Rane wasn't so far gone she didn't realize she could be doing something stupid and dangerous to her well-being. But as long as he kept kissing her, it was almost impossible to keep her feelings in check, to remember why getting into a relationship with this man was too much of a risk.

He broke the kiss, pulling back to meet her gaze, his breath harsh. "You should go upstairs. Now."

Right. There was the voice of reason she needed to hear. He wanted her...obviously. That he had the control to stop made her wonder if he wanted to wait until all the DiNardo crap was behind them. She knew the temptation was too huge and too overwhelming to withstand the pull much longer.

"If you don't want this to go any farther you should go upstairs."

She pushed him back so she could move away from him, nodding as she said, "Right. I'll see you in the morning."

She climbed the stairs, head down, her shoes dangling from her fingers. When she got to her bathroom she peeled off her dress and donned a robe, then used a cleansing cloth to wipe the make-up from her eyes. Her heartbeat hadn't returned to normal, and she could still smell him on her. Her blood still simmered, threatening to heat her body beyond her control into something deeper than she'd ever known.

Blotting her face with a towel, she paused to stare at herself in the mirror. She was being stupid. She wanted Jon, and he wanted her too. Maybe, if she was careful, she could have a relationship with him and still keep a hold on her heart. Since Kyle, she'd been successful with implementing that strategy. Even while she was with Kyle, there had been a part of her she'd held separate and protected. The few relationships she'd had since then had been fun, and she'd ended them before they got complicated.

Pulling the sash tight on her robe, she crossed her bedroom. Cooper was doing his evening ritual in his bed, turning around four or five times before finally settling onto the cushion. Light shone from the bathroom across the hall and she heard water running. Responding to a temptation too strong to resist, she crossed to the open bathroom door and leaned against the jamb.

Unaware of her presence, Jon rinsed his toothbrush before dipping his head to the faucet for a mouthful of water. Wearing only navy flannel pants riding low on his hips, he turned, his motion checked when he caught sight of her. Slowly he reached for a towel. His expression heated before his face went blank.

He dried his face and rehung the towel. "House is locked, alarm is set."

"You're conscientious. Thank you."

His gaze narrowed, and she had the feeling he was trying to figure out whether she was being sarcastic. He must've decided she wasn't. He answered evenly, "You're welcome."

He eyed her as if gauging if he could get through the doorway without touching her. "See you in the morning. Goodnight."

Feeling stronger with her decision, Rane straightened as he moved to go past. She raised a hand and laid it on his chest. He jerked to a stop as if hit by a taser gun, his heart picking up its beat beneath her touch. Distracted by the warm skin, she slid unsteady fingers through golden chest hair.

"Look," he rasped, "I'm trying to do the right thing here."

"Why is us being together not the right thing?"

"Because I don't want to take advantage of the situation. I'm no saint, but I try not to be a jerk."

She studied her hand as she slid it along his chest, tracing the curve of his defined pecs. Then she raised her head and their gazes connected with that same electric current that had been humming between them all evening. "You wouldn't be taking advantage if I want it too."

The corner of his mouth turned up. He caught her hand in his and brought it to his mouth where he nipped at her fingertips. "That's progress. Here's another thing for you to consider, I want more than sex. I want a relationship with you."

"I can't promise more, Jon. I can only do now."

"Can we do now with an option for more?"

"Are we negotiating here?"

"Don't dodge the question."

She huffed out a breath. "Okay, there's an option for more, but that's not a guarantee."

Now his grin flashed. "That's what I wanted to hear. Best damn deal I've ever negotiated."

"Can we get on to the fun stuff now?"

"Hell, yeah, we can get to the fun stuff."

Their mouths met in a kiss that felt as wild as it did desperate. His muscles bunched under her hands as he bent low and scooped her into his arms. He held her securely as his lips found hers again.

The swooniness of the gesture nearly undid her. He broke the kiss and stared into her eyes for a long moment before striding across the hall.

The flameless candles cast her bedroom in shadows. He paused at her bed where the covers were already turned back, pulling her into another seductive kiss filled with tenderness. He set her on the bed, and breaking the kiss, stood with his gaze riveted to where her robe had gaped open to reveal a narrow strip of bare skin. "I wouldn't have been able to resist for so long if I'd know you were naked under that robe."

She reached up to tug at the elastic waistband of his flannels. "Why aren't you naked?"

"'Cause I don't want this over before it starts." He propped his arms on either side of her head, leaning down to press open mouthed kisses to the sensitive skin beneath her ear and along her neck. She could feel his muscles quivering before he finally gave in and lay on top of her: heat pressed to heat, heart pressed to heart.

She trailed her fingers down the dip in his spine, loving the smooth texture of his skin, skimming lightly over the bandage above his hip. She stretched languorously, absorbing the incredible pleasure of his hands and then his lips brushing over her breasts. She slipped a hand under the back waistband of his flannels and ran her hand over his taut buttocks. He moved to the side so he could put his hands to better use, trailing them over her body, stroking and caressing, stoking the heat burning inside her.

She shuddered, and he murmured, "That's it, baby, go with it."

She gasped and reached for him. The liquid pull that had started with that kiss in the kitchen heated to molten, boiling up, until she exploded with a wild, keening moan.

She'd barely regained her equilibrium when he nuzzled her neck, murmuring, "I think we can do that again."

"You trying to kill me?"

"Not kill you. Love you."

The words had her breath hitching, but he didn't give her time to consider the implications. He continued his thorough exploration of her body, but she wanted more of him. She pushed down the elastic waistband of his flannels and sighed with pleasure when she grasped the rigid length of him.

He dropped her forehead to hers, eyes closed, stopping her with his hand over hers. He pushed up from the bed. "Ahh, Rane. I'll be back in a second. I didn't pack a condom when I went brush my teeth."

"I guess I make a better Boy Scout than you. There are a couple in my nightstand."

He looked at her, raising an eyebrow. She smiled. "I lived in hope my dry spell would break."

His grin flashed. "Lucky me." He reached across her to pull open the drawer. When she would have taken the packet from him, he shook his head. "I'll do it. I'm too close to the edge."

He rose to kick off his pants and, with protection taken care of, lowered himself back onto her with a sigh that sounded blissful. "God, that's good." He settled himself firmly into the cradle of her hips. "Really damn good."

For all his intensity, she expected a race to the finish. Instead, he used his hands, his lips, his tongue, stroking and tasting until she felt intoxicated with the feel of him. Her heart beat rapidly in her chest, increasing its pace the more he touched her, and the more she touched him. His muscles shifted under her fingers, flexing or tightening depending on how and where she caressed. They were thorough in their mutual exploration, and her desire peaked, until once again she was on the trembling edge of sanity. When she shifted in anticipation, he held back. "Not yet, sweetheart. You're rushing things. You wouldn't commit to more than tonight, so I'm making this count. There's no rush."

But there was. A long, glorious rush of feeling that nearly overwhelmed her. As much as she wanted more, and now, he took his time to lick and nip at every possible responsive place on her body.

She hadn't known the backs of her knees could be so sensitive. Or the hollow of her collarbone. She'd never had a lover who worshipped her body with such exquisite care. She could do no less than reciprocate, pressing her mouth against the ridge of his shoulder, the dip of his throat, travelling the valley between his pecs and down the ridges of his abs, thrilling as his response grew more urgent. Only when she was trembling and frantic with need, his heavy breathes mirroring hers, did he finally, *finally* enter her with a powerful surge. She caught her breath as sensation shot through her, then released it on a humming sigh.

He framed her face with his hands and built a rhythm steadily rising in intensity, his brilliant blue eyes locked on hers. The kiss they shared deepened as they moved together, finding a pace that felt like a communion. Her need grew, focused and sharp, until teetering at the brink, the last strands of her control snapped sending them both hurdling over the edge. His body tensed and he buried his face in her neck as he followed her into oblivion.

Their breathing evened out as they lay like casualties of war, shell shocked, stranded in no-man's land. Finally, Rane gathered the energy to raise a hand and pat him on the butt. A really delicious, firm butt.

His chest rumbled against her ear when he spoke. "I think I've been blinded. I'll get off so you can breathe. In a minute."

When he did, he wrapped his arm around her so she went with him. She lay sprawled across his body, her legs tangled with his, her head against his shoulder. His warm fingers stroked lazily down the length of her back as she felt the heavy rise of his chest as his breathing deepened. Emotions let loose by their joining settled over her like a warm balm. She wasn't sure she'd be able to push them back into the walled-off corner of her mind to keep her safe.

She'd deal with that later, because right now she wanted to take this little slice of heaven and hold on tight.

She cuddled into him, comforted by the secure feeling of his arms around her, and she allowed herself to drift into sleep.

Chapter Ten

Rane woke to Cooper's nose resting on the edge of her pillow. He stared at her with unblinking eyes. On the other side of the bed lay rumpled blankets and an indentation on the pillow. Where was Jon? This was going to be awkward if he'd gone back to his bed. Maybe he'd gone to work and left her sleeping.

Sitting up, she gave Cooper an absent pet, then took a moment to rest her head in her hands. *Get a grip*, she told herself. She and Jon had made love. *No.* Despite what he'd said, they'd had sex. Really stupendous sex. She wasn't committing to anything more than that.

What had he meant when he'd said "Not kill you. Love you?" "Love you" as in making love to you, or "love you" as in I love you? She admitted to feeling a bit freaked out. He'd made that claim, then she'd spent the night wrapped around him. She needed to be careful or she wouldn't be able to keep the distance she needed to survive the devastation when he left.

He'd leave. She was sure of it. Not next week, maybe even not next month, but at some point, he'd realize she had too much baggage he didn't want to unpack.

Deciding she really, *really* needed coffee and a shower, and in that order, she pulled on sweatpants and a thermal shirt, and after taking care of business in the bathroom, headed downstairs.

She came to an abrupt stop at the doorway to the kitchen. The storm had cleared, and sunlight streamed into the room. Jon stood barefoot and bare chested, a spatula in his hand, flipping pancakes. Man, oh man, he looked way more tempting than the pancakes. She tried to tell herself it was the lack of coffee that made her weak in the knees, but when he turned toward her and flashed that lightning grin, she knew it was all him. "Hey."

***

Jon looked up to see Rane leaning against the door jamb. She looked uncertain, like she didn't know what to expect from him. Which suited him fine. It was okay to keep her wondering. Stepping back from the stove, he crossed to where she stood, dipped his head and gave her a quick good morning kiss. He pulled back and tipped up her chin. "Don't overthink it, sweetheart."

"I'm not overthinking anything."

"Yeah you are. I can see the little wheels spinning behind your eyes."

She shrugged, looking like a sullen teenager.

"Grab the butter and syrup. These are about ready."

She did as he asked, filled her coffee mug, and they sat at the table, pancakes piled on a platter between them. He stepped away and jogged up the stairs, returning wearing a black t-shirt. He shrugged at her raised eyebrows. "Mom wouldn't let me or Nathan sit at the table without a shirt. Old habits die hard."

"Good mom," she said. Rane speared a couple of pancakes and laid them on her plate then watched with wide eyes as he drowned his pancakes in syrup. She dipped her forkful of pancake into the small pool of syrup on the side of her plate and took a bite. "These are really good."

"Don't look so surprised. Pancakes are a specialty."

Cooper sat beside Jon's chair, eager dog eyes watching Jon's every move.

She considered Cooper, then Jon. "Have you been feeding him at the table?"

"Huh? Me? That would be bad, right?"

"Yes, that would be bad. I don't want him learning to beg."

Jon cast a regretful look at the dog. "Sorry, pal. The lady says no, so that means no." Cooper collapsed into a sorrowful heap and Jon frowned. "You're not his favorite person right now, you know that?"

"Yeah. One of us has to be the grown up. You can give him a pancake after we're done. He has a weakness for them."

Jon studied Rane as he ate. He couldn't get enough of her. The memories from their night together pulsed between them. The sleepy sexy awareness in her sea green eyes and the slightly rumpled look from being well loved...he thought she looked damned perfect.

He could get used to this. To waking with her next to him in bed, to sitting across from her at breakfast. But there were matters, serious matters, that needed taking care of before he could advance their relationship to where he wanted it to go. He swallowed his last bite of pancake and sat back, his gaze on her as he sipped his coffee. "You're meeting with Kyle today. We need to talk about that."

"I'm not sure what there is to talk about." She fiddled with her fork before spearing a triangle of pancake. "Something was bothering me after I talked with him the other night."

"What's that?"

"He knew who you were and that you were coming to pick me up. He seems to know my schedule. He knew when I got off work that evening, and that I'm scheduled for today."

Jon nodded. "We've confirmed the DiNardos have an inside person at St. Augie's. It's the same person that's stealing the Oxy. We're working on nailing down who it is. Nathan got a lead when he was a patient."

"Really? While he was recovering from a bullet wound he figured out who the inside guy is? Talk about multi-tasking."

"Yeah, he's pretty motivated about this case." He pushed his plate to the side. "What time is your lunch break?"

"Three, unless we get swamped."

"Okay. I worked it out with the team. Since Kyle knows who I am, Ty and Ben will be at the picnic benches when you come out. They'll be wearing maintenance staff shirts. I've got a couple other guys from the division who'll be hanging out in the area. We'll have you wired. If DiNardo tries anything, and I mean *anything* Rane, I want you to—"

"Wired?" she interrupted. "I won't be wired."

"Yeah, you will. It's not a big deal. I'll be in an unmarked car listening. This is important to build our case. If things go sideways, we'll be right on top of it."

"No. No way, Jon. I can't wear a wire."

"Why not?"

She appeared flustered, and he wondered why she seemed to be scrambling for a reason. "I'd feel too weird. Too unnatural. Kyle knows me well enough to realize if my behavior is off." She got up to top off his coffee, then hers. When she leaned against the counter and sipped from her mug, he figured the distance meant she was trying to hide her anxiety.

"You'll be fine. I'll set you up this morning so you can get used to it. By three you won't even remember it's there."

"I'll remember, and I can't wear a wire in the hospital. I have to think about patient confidentiality. No wire, Jon."

He swore silently under his breath, then rose to stand in front of her, legs apart, arms folded. "How am I supposed to keep you safe if you don't cooperate?"

"I am cooperating. I told you about this meeting. I won't wear a wire. You didn't see him the other day. He wasn't threatening. He's not going to hurt me."

"You're putting a lot of faith in a guy fresh out of prison for a major drug offense." He saw a flicker in her expression and his instincts hummed. She was hiding something. He tagged that, then continued. "Kyle DiNardo is a known heroin supplier and is a key member of the area's largest illegal drug organization." And was the only serious boyfriend she'd ever had.

"He won't hurt me," she repeated. "I won't wear a wire."

Jon spun around to pace the kitchen. Frustration, jealousy, fear for her safety—they made a lousy combination. Cooper sat at attention with his ears perked. Jon returned to the table for a pancake. He threw it like a Frisbee. The dog snagged it and swallowed it in one mouthful.

Rane sipped her coffee as Jon paced. He was in a no-win situation. The wire was non-negotiable. That had come from Denton. If she was worried about acting self-conscious because she was wired, then the solution was that she wouldn't know it was there. He hated deceiving her, and she'd be pissed if she found out he'd planted a bug, but he'd deal with that. Keeping her safe beat out lying to her.

"He better not hurt you."

"He won't and thanks for not pushing. I'm going up for my shower. I'll straighten the kitchen when I come down."

Jon shoved back his concerns about the coming meeting. She was here with him now and he wanted her with a hunger honed sharper by the night they'd spent together. What he felt for her was more than he'd ever felt for another woman, and it colored every interaction with her. Catching her eye, he gripped his shirt by the back of the collar and pulled it over his head and was gratified when she swallowed audibly. Her gaze lowered to his chest as he tossed the shirt aside.

"Good idea." He saw her eyes go a deeper green when he took a step toward her.

"What is?"

"Taking a shower."

Her smile lit her eyes. "Are you thinking a shower for two?"

"That's the idea."

He cupped her face, fingers threading into the silky hair at the nape of her neck as he took her mouth in a slow, deep kiss. She tasted of maple syrup and sweetened coffee, the combination making him want to slurp her up in one tasty gulp.

Her arms tightened around his shoulders, and when he reached down for her, she wrapped her legs around his hips. He boosted her up, lips still locked, and carried her up the stairs.

***

Rane exited the hospital employee entrance carrying her lunchbox. The sun shone a brilliant deep blue, reminding her why she loved Seattle. She still felt the tingle from her and Jon's shared shower. God, the man made her feel. Everything was *more* with him in her life. More color, more heat, more emotion. She couldn't be in love with him. She *wouldn't* let herself love him. Their relationship couldn't go anywhere. She knew that. She'd enjoy what he gave her in the moment. She sighed. If she wasn't going to blow this meeting with Kyle she'd better focus.

She approached the picnic tables, scanning for him. He wasn't there. She spotted the "maintenance men" and recognized Ben and Ty wearing matching shirts and caps. She deliberately chose a table far enough from where they sat so they wouldn't be able to eavesdrop. She unpacked her lunch and took a sip from her bottle of Diet Pepsi. She was chewing her first bite of Caesar salad when Kyle slid onto the bench across the table from her.

He hunched into his pea coat despite the unseasonably warm temperature, his gaze furtively scanning the area. "Your cop friend around?"

"No." He gave a small grin, a reminder of the shy young man he'd once been. She had a twinge of nostalgia, but whatever had been between them was long gone.

"What's going on, Kyle?"

"You need to leave town before something happens to you." His gaze continued to sweep the area and she wondered what he was watching for.

His nervousness made her wary. "Why would something happen to me?"

"Simon's not going to let you out of this alive. He's using you." Kyle's eyes, shades darker than his brother's, focused on her.

"I know he wants me to inform on the task force. To let him know what they're up to. He threatened me. I told him I'd do it. I don't like it, but I'll do it."

Kyle gave a harsh laugh. "You think that's all there is to it? Simon's got the perfect setup. He keeps me in line by threatening to hurt you. He keeps you in line by threatening to hurt your old man. Once he's dealt with the cops, you're done. He'll kill your old man, and he'll kill you."

"My dad has Alzheimer's. He's not a threat. I'm doing what Simon asked of me. In fact, you can tell him the task force is planning to raid a stash house on South Dearborn tonight."

"That won't be enough. It doesn't matter that your dad's mind is shot. It's payback. Your dad framed me and sent me to prison, so he has to be punished. You, you're even more important because, in Simon's mind, you're responsible for setting me against the family, for making me want something more than a place in the family business. He can't forgive you for that." Kyle paused and Rane suppressed a shudder. "He's been planning this for a long time."

"Then you're in danger, too, aren't you? By coming here and telling me all this, you're putting yourself in danger. If Simon finds out, he'll see you talking to me as being disloyal to him and the family."

"I'll deal with Simon. Listen to me, Rane. I'm serious. You have to break it off with the cop. Get your dad and get out of town. I can give you money if you need it. I'll come for you when all this ends and we can be together. Simon will bring down the task force, he's got a plan. I'll deal with him when I can. But to do that I need you out of the way, to know you're safe."

She looked at the turbulent expression on the face of the man she'd cared about a long time ago. She spoke carefully. "Kyle, you know we can't be together. You should leave. Get out of Seattle before you get sucked back into the business. You could find somewhere to live away from the here. Go to college, become a carpenter, whatever. Make a new life for yourself."

He shook his head. "I can't. Maybe later, but not now. I've got to take care of some things first." His expression turned bleak. "This is my life. It's my fault you were dragged into it. It was naïve to've thought I could have a normal life with you back then. I'm older now, and smarter. I can get us out of this."

"We were young, Kyle. It was as much my fault as yours. My dad made a choice that made the situation worse." She swallowed. "I'm sorry for that. I know that doesn't do a thing to erase the time you spent in prison, but I'm sorry for what my dad did."

He hitched up a shoulder in a shrug. "He was protecting you. That's what good dads do."

***

Denton locked gazes with Jon. "What the hell?"

"Fuck," Jon swore.

The smell of rotting garbage came through the open window of the unmarked police car as they sat in an alley a block from the hospital, Rane's conversation with Kyle DiNardo came through the speaker on Jon's phone loud and clear. Denton leaned back in the passenger seat, a frown creasing his forehead as he sipped from his takeout coffee cup. "When we get back to the station, you're looking into the bust that sent DiNardo to prison. Figure out what the hell she was talking about. We need to know exactly what happened." He cocked his head, a *don't fuck with me* expression on his face. "This getting personal between you and Rane Smith?"

Jon drummed his fingers on the steering wheel. "Yeah, it's personal."

When he was pissed, Denton had a way of looking at a man that about cut him in half. "If you can't be objective, I'm pulling you. I won't risk what this team's been working on for so long if you can't handle it."

"I'll handle it."

"You'd better. And Jon? It looks like your girl is hiding something."

***

After a couple hours of serious digging and talking with a cop who'd been involved in Kyle DiNardo's arrest, Jon figured he knew what Rane was hiding. He rubbed his temple where a headache had taken up residence with a pounding that felt like hammer blows. He pulled out his phone and punched the first number on speed dial. She should've been home from work by now, but she wasn't picking up. The slightly husky voice he found incredibly sexy asked him to leave a message. "Rane, call me." He sent the same message in a text.

He threw down his phone and sat back at his desk, fingers tapping a beat on his knee. At nine-thirty in the evening, the station was quiet. As they'd expected, the tip Rane had given Kyle had been passed on and the DiNardos had cleared the stash house by the time the team arrived. As a precaution, they'd sent in a robot to check for boobytraps. Good thing. It'd detected a bomb attached to a tripwire. The construction had been slipshod and the device quickly defused. It'd all seemed too easy. That, and the fact that Rane should have answered her phone, made him uneasy.

He made another call, this time punching the second number on his favorites list.

"What?" A lot of irritation was packed into that one word.

"Shitty mood?"

"JonJon, thank God. Mom keeps calling to see how I'm doing."

"She can't stand that you won't let her come take care of you."

"I'm going crazy sitting in this apartment, but she'd send me permanently around the bend. Tell me what's going on."

Nathan's tone evened out as they talked about the case. "Douglas Smith framed DiNardo? That's a pretty serious charge against a cop who had a long and spotless record."

"Yeah, it's fucked up, but that's what it's looking like."

"Explain."

Jon had to admire his brother's capacity to cut to the chase. "DiNardo went to prison for possession with intent to distribute. Two pounds of black tar were found under the back seat of his car."

Arranging the information in his head to explain to Nathan helped him see it more clearly. "At the time, DiNardo was trafficking heroin sourced from Afghanistan and shipped through Europe."

"That's the pretty white stuff. Black tar comes up from Mexico."

"Yeah. And guess what? Two kilos of black tar went missing from the evidence room of a precinct across town."

"What makes you think it was Smith? Anyone could have planted it."

Jon sat back with a sigh, his chair making a squeaking sound that arrowed straight to where the hammers were pounding. "I planted a bug on her so I could hear the conversation with Kyle."

Nathan let out a long laugh. "She'll roast your balls when she finds out."

"She won't find out."

"The hell she won't. You won't be able to keep that from her. You're honest to a fault, man. You'll tell her." He paused. "What'd you hear?"

Trying to think past the headache, and burying the worry that his brother was right, he went on. "She told Kyle she was sorry about what her old man had done. Whatever it was resulted in DiNardo going to prison, but he seems to have dealt with it. He was more concerned about keeping her safe from his sociopathic brother. Says Simon means to kill her. He wanted her to leave town with her dad and he'd join up with them later."

"She didn't jump at the chance?"

Jon didn't bother responding. He pulled open his desk drawer and found a bottle of Tylenol. He put the phone on speaker and set it on his desk so he could wrestle with the child-proof lid. He thought about Kyle telling Rane they could still be together. She'd nixed that idea, but their history grated on him. She'd cared about Kyle. What if she still had a thing for him? First loves were the hardest to get over, weren't they? Finally wrangling the cap off, Jon shook out a couple pills and tossed them in his mouth, chasing them down with a swallow of cold coffee.

Nathan's voice sounded tinny over the phone. "You know this means she could be prosecuted for withholding evidence. How will we keep her from being charged?"

Jon leaned back in the chair and gave silent thanks for his brother. No matter how much Nathan goaded him, his brother always had his back. "Yeah, I know. I'll do whatever it takes to keep her in the clear. Best bet is the DA using Rane to testify against the DiNardos. He'll waive charges if she can help nail them."

"What was Doug Smith's motive? To get Kyle away from Rane?"

"Maybe. But there's another angle that I'm looking into. A guy who worked with Smith claims Kyle was cheating on Rane with another woman who ended up dead."

"Dead how?"

"Strangled, with heroin in her system. At the time, the cops tried but couldn't pin it on Kyle. The guy I talked to said Smith believed it was Kyle, but others thought it more likely that Simon had killed her." Jon paused, thinking about Nathan's Savannah. He cleared his throat and went on. "Upshot is, Smith knew the DiNardos were bad, and that hanging with Kyle put Rane in danger. I don't know if I'd do anything different if it were my daughter."

"You would. You'd never frame someone. Me, on the other hand? If it protected someone I loved, I would do it and damn the consequences."

Jon gave a humorless laugh, then shifted gears. "You feel up to taking a drive?"

"Hell, yeah."

"I'll pick you up in ten."

Chapter Eleven

Glad to be back home after a tiring shift that had gone into overtime, Rane pulled up the hood of her jacket. She slammed the car door and bolted through the pounding rain to the kitchen door. Lightning flashed and thunder cracked like it would split open the sky. She opened the kitchen door and flipped the light switch. Nothing. The porchlight had been out, too. Power outages weren't uncommon during these intense storms, especially in older neighborhoods. Using her phone as a flashlight, she set her purse and lunchbox on the counter. Cooper always greeted her at the door, but thunder freaked him out and he was probably under her bed. She moved through the dark house, calling the dog. Fighting back nerves, she followed the beam of light up the stairs, crouching down to peer under her bed. No Cooper. She felt a sudden chill. What if the power wasn't out because of the storm? She tried to remember if neighboring houses had been dark when she'd driven up the street. What if Kyle or Simon was in the house? Dread tightened her chest and she turned to her closet to get the .45 from the lockbox. She'd get the gun, then find Cooper, and then call Jon.

"Hello, cupcake. Remember me?"

Alarm skated up her spine at the sinister voice. She turned to face the man standing in the shadowed corner behind the door, the light from her phone glinting dully off a gun pointed at her heart. Short, stocky, with hair cut close to his head, it was the man from the grocery store parking lot, the man she'd pepper sprayed. Simon's goon.

"What are you doing here? Jon will be home any minute now." Her gaze kept returning to the gun in his hand.

"Don't fucking try to bluff me. We got eyes on Garretson. He's at the police station. Boss wants to see you." He motioned with the gun. "Let's go."

"Go where?"

"Where I tell you."

She held herself motionless, mind racing over the possibilities for escape. Every idea that flashed through her mind came up against the reality of the gun pointed at her. She tried to assure herself that if Simon wanted to see her, pepper-spray guy wasn't likely to shoot her. "What does he want, and what did you do to my dog?"

He ignored the first question. "Dog is taking a little nap. Boss said it'd be okay to kill him, but me, I like dogs. Gave him some pills in a wad of sandwich meat and he was out." He motioned again with the gun. "Move it. You don't cooperate and I'll be happy to put a hole in an arm or leg. You fucking tear gassed me. I don't care what the boss says, I owe you. Give me your phone."

Reluctantly, she handed it over and he shoved it into his pocket, reaching into his coat to pull out a different phone. He must've been in her house for a while because his coat was dry. He texted, then returned the phone to his pocket.

"I want to see Cooper." She refused to appear cowed. She was terrified but she'd be damned before she let him know it.

He pocketed her phone and pulled out a small flashlight to illuminate the doorway. "The dog is downstairs."

The goon's dark presence gave her the creeps as he followed her down the stairs.

"He's by the couch."

She crossed the shadowed living room. Pepper-spray guy held the light down so it only illuminated the floor. She guessed he didn't want it to be seen from the window.

She spotted Cooper lying next to the couch and rushed forward, dropping to her knees beside him. Running her hands over the still form, her fear eased when she felt the steady rise and fall of his chest. "What did you give him?"

"Enough to knock him out. Now let's go. Boss will be here in a minute."

She recognized the chime of her phone from his pocket. He took it out and tossed it onto the couch.

She remained crouched next to Cooper, her fingers tightening in his fur. "How do I know you won't hurt me?" She held her voice steady.

"You'll have to take your chances. You don't move now, cupcake, I will hurt you, and swear to God, I'll enjoy it."

With the muzzle of the gun prodding her, they passed through the kitchen and out the door. She watched as he moved to her electrical box at the side of the house and flipped some switches. "Wouldn't want anyone to be suspicious that the electricity isn't on, now would we?" Light from the kitchen shone through the window, making her wish she were safe inside.

The rain still fell in sheets, though the heart of the storm seemed to have moved south where thunder rumbled in the distance. They walked down the driveway. Headlights reflected from the wet pavement as a vehicle drove slowly up to the street. For a moment, Rane feared that Jon had returned home. The guy holding a gun to her back could shoot him before he even got out of his truck. The black SUV that pulled to a stop in front of them looked the same as the one she'd been thrown into in the grocery store parking lot.

With the gun pushing her forward, pepper-spray guy opened the front passenger door, pushed her in, then climbed into the backseat.

She gripped the armrest and stared at the man in the driver's seat. Once again, she was seated next to Simon DiNardo. As always, he'd dressed in such a way as to make himself unremarkable. No witness—if they could see inside this blacked-out vehicle—would be able to say he looked anything but average.

"Rane, Nice of you to join me."

"Like I had a choice." A warning sound chimed.

"True, you didn't, but let's try to have a civilized conversation. Please, buckle your seatbelt." He faced forward and began driving.

She snapped the seatbelt in place, abandoning the idea jumping out of the SUV. "You're making a mistake, Simon. This is kidnapping. Let me go and I won't tell anyone."

He gave a humorless laugh. Rain spattered against the windshield with a steady thudding, windshield wipers barely keeping up.

"Where are you taking me?"

"For a drive around the city. No need to be alarmed. You'll be back safe and sound within the hour." When she didn't move, he sighed. "I didn't hurt you last time, did I? I frequently conduct business from my car. I find if I keep moving it's harder for individuals like the Garretsons to find me."

She crossed her arms over her chest, trying to suppress the shaking that now threatened to wrack her entire body. Simon flat out terrified her and she didn't know if she would come out of this alive.

"This little adventure we're going on tonight, Rane, is to help you understand clearly that I'm in charge, and you are to follow my orders."

"I know you're in charge, Simon." She would tell him what he wanted to hear, anything to return home unharmed. "I've been doing what you told me to do. I've even been included in meetings with the task force. I passed Kyle the tip about the stash house."

Simon drove precisely at the speed limit through the darkened streets, using his blinkers at every turn. "Which is why you're still useful to me." They approached St. Augustine's and Simon slowed to turn into the employee parking lot. He backed into an unmarked space in a dimly lit corner and let the engine idle.

"What are we doing here?"

He pointed to the parking garage across the street. "Hardly anybody parks on the top two levels. My man was up there this afternoon, watching you through the scope of a rifle. Not a soul came by. He had you in the crosshairs from the moment you stepped out of the hospital door and all the time you were eating and talking to Kyle. He could have squeezed off a round so easily and been gone before the cops figured out where the shot had come from. I told my guy to let you live." Her breath hitched at the cold, callous way he described having her killed.

She sat stock still, the car's heater did nothing to touch the cold suffusing her body.

Simon put the car in gear and pulled out of the space. Their next stop was her father's care facility. Parked on the street, avoiding the wash of a streetlight outside the fenced area where residents could sit outside on sunny days, Simon said, "Killing your father would be so easy it's almost embarrassing." He spoke as if reading a grocery list. "I could have someone poison him, slip something in with his daily meds, or set up over there." He motioned across the street to a multi-story apartment complex, "The third or fourth floors would give the best angle. Aim for the back of his head and squeeze the trigger nice and smooth. It would be doing him a favor, really."

She could visualize it clearly and her body shook with fear. She wished she was wearing a heavier coat and gloves. "I get it. At your say-so, you could kill me. my dad, or my dog." She hated Simon with every fiber of her being. "I'll keep doing what you want me to do."

"Good. Now listen carefully. I wasn't happy to learn you met with Kyle today. You're not to meet with him again. I want him to concentrate on the business."

She nodded jerkily.

He turned his head and those cold pale eyes glared at her. "He might have given you the impression you have a choice about reporting what the task force is doing, that there's a way out. You don't and there isn't. If you want to stay alive, and your father to stay alive, you'll carry on as I wish." He paused and she wished he would drive so he wouldn't be able to look at her. "Is that clear?"

"Perfectly."

"Good. Next, you're to tell the Garretson brothers I want to meet with them."

"I will, but I can't make them agree to meet." She wished the shaking would stop. If Simon had wanted to kill her, she'd already be dead. Objectively, she knew she didn't need to be afraid, but she couldn't stop her body's response.

"My guess is they never told the task force about their real motive for hunting me down. Tell them I'll keep what I know about Savannah quiet, but they need to meet with me."

"Who's Savannah?"

"Why don't you ask them? She's the reason they've been dogging my heels all these years. It's time they realized that their little secret might not stay a secret. Tell them it'll be only me and them. I have information that will allow them to put away kingpins in major drug smuggling organizations from Canada to Mexico and to seize enough product to make world news. I'll let you know the time and place.

"And Rane? Make it clear they're to come alone. No wires and no backup or they get nothing."

"They won't believe it. They won't believe you'd give up your empire. Why would you?"

"Let's say I'm rethinking the family business model. I want immunity for my people."

"I'll tell them."

A car pulled up behind them. Simon glanced at the rearview mirror. His phone vibrated and he checked the screen before turning back to her. "When we talk they'll see that I mean it." He shrugged. "If they take the offer, they'll come off as heroes. That can't be helped, but I'll get what I want. My family will be safe." He tipped his head toward the back seat. "Mick will drive you back to your house."

Simon opened the door and stepped out into the rain. In the headlights behind them, she saw him get into that vehicle.

Pepper-spray Mick took the driver's seat and in minutes they were cruising back to her neighborhood.

***

Jon sat in his truck with the engine idling, waiting outside Nathan's apartment building. He tried Rane's phone again. Nothing. Okay, now he was past worried. He switched to a tracking app. It had taken some convincing, but she had finally agreed to download it onto her phone on the condition he only use it if he thought she was in danger. It pulled up a map and a little blinking red dot showed her location. She was at home. His worry decreased marginally.

Nathan pulled open the truck door and climbed into the passenger seat. "I just got off the phone with Mom. Again."

Jon grinned. "Better you than me, bro." They both adored their mother, but as she had a tendency to fixate on the dangers associated with being a cop, keeping her at an emotional distance on this topic was best for all of them.

"You have no idea. It was all I could do to convince her she didn't need to fly up here. I finally had to talk to Dad. Lindy expecting to deliver within the month helped because no way would Mom miss that."

"Hard to believe little sister is having her second kid."

"Isn't she still fifteen?"

Jon laughed. "Feels like she should be." He joined the traffic on the boulevard, passing St. Augustine's. "Has the beautiful Lily been making you all better?"

"She made me all better yesterday, but had to work today. I couldn't convince her to play hooky," he said with a grin. "We going to your girlfriend's place? Or should I say your place, since you're shacked up?"

"Fuck you," Jon told him mildly.

Nathan gave a short laugh. "Well?"

"Yeah, we're going to Rane's place. She's not answering her cell but the locator shows she's there. I want to make sure she's okay, then we're meeting Eddie. It's late, but he says he's got something for us and I don't want to take a chance he'll go on a bender and forget whatever he thinks he has."

At Nathan's nod Jon drove up to the house that was beginning to feel like home. As always, he scanned the neighborhood for anything out of place. Eddie, their informant, wasn't the most reliable of sources, but he'd said he had something on Simon and Jon didn't like keeping that information on ice. Nonetheless, he felt an urgency to see Rane. To touch her, to know she was safe. He wouldn't relax until he had actual physical contact. He also wanted to talk to her about what she'd said to Kyle, about what he'd found out about her father. But Denton had told him to wait, so he'd wait.

Denton figured it was possible Rane was playing both sides, that she was telling Simon more than what they wanted her to. Jon knew she was being straight with them, but he'd have to wait to get all the details from her. That she hadn't told him about Doug Smith's involvement from the get-go bothered him. Competing loyalties were never a good thing.

He parked in the driveway and saw a light on in the kitchen. They got out of the truck and he pulled out his key to open the side door. Nathan followed him into the kitchen where Rane's purse sat on the counter with her keys and lunchbox. Guessing she was upstairs, he called out, "Rane, it's me. Nathan's here, too."

Silence. He crossed the dining room to the base of the stairs. "Rane?" Maybe she was in the shower. He glanced at his brother. "I'll be down in a minute."

He took the stairs two at a time, fear compelling him to move faster. Turning on lights, he checked her bedroom, then the master bath. No Rane. Where the hell was she? Where was Cooper?

"Jon, you better get down here."

He charged down the stairs. Nathan had turned on a light in the living room and crouched next to the coffee table. Jon rounded the couch, dread balling in his chest. The dog lay motionless on the floor.

Nathan lay a hand on the still form. "He's alive. I think he's been drugged."

Jon went to his knees, feeling the dog for injuries. Cooper breathed slowly and deeply. "You're right." That ball of dread grew to choke him. He rose swiftly to his feet. "He's got her. That shit DiNardo has Rane. Let's go."

Nathan put a hand on his arm, grip tight. "Pull it back. I'm not usually the one to be saying it, but we need to think this through. First thing, we notify the team."

"You can call them from the truck. We've got to go. We're getting her back."

"Without a doubt. Let's do it without getting her killed. We think this through and follow a plan. We don't even know where she is."

"The bastard probably took her to their compound." The DiNardos had property on the outskirts of the city where a collection of buildings covered several wooded acres. He didn't particularly care that it was surrounded by security fencing and monitored by cameras. That wouldn't have stopped him in Afghanistan and it wouldn't stop him here.

He jerked free from his brother's grip. "I won't sit on my hands and wait for the team to make a plan. That'll give DiNardo more time to be ready for us. Or to hurt her."

"You're not going off half-cocked either. First thing, we need to go over this place."

"Shit, Nate. He's got my girl."

"Yeah. He's got her because she's your girl. My bet is he took her to get to you. He'll use you to get to me, if he can. I'm the one who took a slice out of his face. The team doesn't know about Savannah, but Simon does, and he knows we won't let up on him because of her. We'll go after Rane, but we go after her with a plan that keeps all of us alive."

"Fuck." Jon dragged his fingers through his hair. "You're right." He breathed deep, fighting back the urge to storm the DiNardo stronghold, guns blazing. He spotted Rane's cell on the couch and grabbed it. "Go ahead and call the team. I'll see what I can find here." Rane didn't even have a locked screen. While Nathan stood with his phone to his ear, Jon swiped through recent email messages and texts but found nothing relevant. Nothing to indicate where she'd gone or who she might have left with. It struck him suddenly that she might not be with Simon at all, that she might have left with Kyle. Even if she had, it wouldn't have been voluntarily, he was sure of it. She would never have left her unconscious dog or her phone unless forced to.

Nathan pocketed his phone. "Denton says to stay put until they get here."

Jon prowled the living room. He wanted to be out there, searching for Rane. To make sure she was safe. Why had he let her meet with Kyle in the first place? He should have–

A knock sounded at the front door and he froze. An instant later he was across the room and swinging the door open. Rane rushed into his arms and instinctively he caught her, pulling her into a rough embrace.

"Are you okay? Where the hell have you been?" The fear that had been clawing at his throat eased, replaced by a relief so great it made him shaky. He loosened his grip enough to tip back her head. Huge green eyes stood out from her pale face. "Rane, what happened? Are you okay?"

She shook her head and gave a shuddering sigh as she tucked her head and burrowed into him.

Wrapping his arms around her, he held tight.

Chapter Twelve

Jon held Rane close for a long minute before she finally pushed back. "Is Cooper all right?"

Reluctantly, Jon loosened his grip, then reached out to push the door shut. She let go of him to cross to where the dog lay on the floor.

"I think he's okay," Nathan said as she stroked the dog's head. "He needs to sleep it off."

"Poor baby," she crooned. "If he doesn't come around soon I'm taking him to the emergency vet clinic."

"What happened?" Jon crouched beside her. "Where were you?"

Sitting on the floor, fingers buried in Cooper's brown fur, Rane wore an expression he couldn't read. "Mick was here when I got home from work, Simon's guy I pepper-sprayed that night outside the supermarket." She gave a humorless laugh. "I'd finally convinced you I didn't need you to drive me back and forth and then Simon sent Mick. He was waiting inside."

Jon's anger caught fire. "How'd he get in?"

She shrugged, defeat in the gesture. "He cut the power and disarmed the alarm. He was here and Cooper was knocked out."

"What happened?"

"He had a gun, so I didn't have any choice but to do as he said. He took my phone and told me we were going for a ride with Simon. When I got in the SUV—the same one from before—Simon said I needed a little incentive, that he wanted to show me something." She sat quietly for a moment. The haunted expression on her face pulling on every protective instinct Jon possessed. "Apparently, Simon's angry at Kyle for meeting with me. Simon said he didn't want me to get the wrong impression in case Kyle might've given me the idea that I have a choice about cooperating with him."

Cooper blinked his eyes open and Rane bent forward. "Oh, there you are, my boy. There you are. You're okay, baby." She crooned the words and stroked her dog's head before looking back at Jon.

"What'd he mean that you needed a little incentive?" Nathan asked as he eased himself down onto the couch.

She shrugged. "He drove to St. Augustine's and pointed out where he said one of his guys waited with a scoped rifle when I was meeting with Kyle. Simon told me any day he wanted, he could shoot me when I was in the parking lot. Then he drove us by my dad's facility. He knows when the nurses bring the patients outside, and showed me vantage points where someone could hide and shoot."

Jon clenched his fists. "The fucking bastard. I'll tear him apart until he's nothing more than little pieces." He nearly choked on the words from the rage surging through him, nearly blinding him.

He took a deep breath—even his lungs were clenched—as the image of Rane, shot by a sniper, flashed across his mind. In Afghanistan, he'd seen what a bullet shot from a high-powered rifle could do to a person, and he'd be damned if he'd let that happen to Rane. He forced himself to clamp down on the fury, to search for the calm he'd need if he was going to get Simon and keep Rane alive...and stay alive himself.

Jon stood and began pacing, reaching for control.

Nathan rose to stand in front of him, his movements stiff, reminding Jon that his brother had been shot.

He stopped pacing and addressed Nathan. "The team should be here any minute. Rane can stay with them while we go find Eddie. We'll see what he's got in case it can help us, and then we'll go after the DiNardos. Simon's always been a homebody so most likely he's at the compound. Odds are Kyle's there with him. We can take them both out."

"You can't do that." Rane's voice sounded strained.

"The hell we can't." He'd gotten himself under control. The way he needed to be to carry out his mission. "He had you kidnapped, and threatened you with the intent to scare the hell out of you. We're going after him."

She shook her head, shoulders rigid. "Simon wants to meet with you. Only you and Nathan, not the team. He says he wants to talk about Savannah."

She looked from him to his brother, her confusion evident.

It was Nathan who spoke in the sudden silence. "Why the hell should we do that? Savannah's dead, he killed her. There's nothing to talk about."

"He says he'll give you information on other bad guys in the illegal drug trade. It sounds like he wants to make a deal that will take the heat off him and his family." She paused. "Who's Savannah?"

"An old memory." Nathan's features tightened.

A vehicle pulled up outside, car doors slammed and Jon crossed the room to open the door. The rest of the team filed into the house, forestalling any revelations that might've been forthcoming.

***

Denton crouched next to Rane, his massive shoulders blocking the rest of the room. "How's this guy doing?"

Cooper had perked up a little at the strangers coming into the house, but was still pretty much out of it. "He's coming around."

Denton reached out a hand to stroke the dog's ears before standing. He nodded to Jon. "Tell me what's going on."

While Jon related the events of the evening, anger lining his every word and gesture, Rane had the sudden intuition that Simon could be playing them. There was a history between Simon and the Garretson brothers, a history that had to do with the mysterious Savannah, and Rane didn't believe for a second that Simon would honor any deal he made. Maybe he was trying to buy time and divert the team from their goal by dangling the prize of a huge bust. Regardless, Simon was playing his game and only he knew the rules.

With a few expletives to describe the Mick and Simon DiNardo, Jon finished filling in Denton and the team.

Denton nodded abruptly. "You and Ben go see Eddie, see what he's got."

"Then we'll bring in DiNardo on kidnapping charges," Jon stated.

"Not tonight, you won't." At Jon's angry look Denton continued explaining, his voice calm. "We'll add that to the long list of charges we'll eventually pin on him, but we're not jeopardizing our time, effort, and taxpayers' money by rushing this. We'll go after him when we're ready, and not before."

"I'm going with Jon to see Eddie."

Denton glared at Nathan. "You're staying with me. You haven't been cleared to return to duty so you're damn lucky all I'm doing is taking you home."

When Nathan looked ready to argue Denton cut him off. "I get he's your brother and you two stick like glue, but I could bust your ass for conducting police work without medical clearance."

"All I did was go with my brother to his girlfriend's house. That's not police work," Nathan said calmly. "Now all I'm doing is planning on a chat with a friend." Rane got a funny feeling to be called Jon's girlfriend. She wasn't sure if it was a good funny or a bad funny, but she was glad to see Denton didn't bat an eyelash over their relationship and figured Jon must've told him.

"Not happening. Ben goes with Jon. Ty," Denton pointed to the other man, "call Bricker and see if he came up with anything in those financials on Simon DiNardo he was going through. It's late but call him anyway."

While Denton gave out assignments, Jon crossed the room to where Rane sat next to Cooper. He reached down a hand. "Come with me."

She let him pull her to her feet. "Where?"

He didn't answer, instead leading her down the darkened hall. When they were out of sight of everyone, he pulled her into his arms and he lowered his head. The kiss scorched her mouth. Intense, wild, and deep, she had to grip his shoulders to stay upright. Her fingers dug into hard muscle that bunched under her touch. All the emotions that had been building inside her like a pressure cooker exploded when Jon hit the release valve.

She responded to him with a need so acute she felt overwhelmed. He pulled her up until her hips cradled against his, her breasts pressed against his chest, and their lips and tongues devoured each other, taking in the sustenance needed to go on. Long minutes passed before he broke the mind-altering kiss. In the dim light she could see him making an effort to rein the emotions coursing through him. His fingers tangled in her hair while his thumbs stroked along her jaw. He drew in an unsteady breath then rested his forehead against hers, melting her heart. "You okay?"

"I am now." Her arms encircled his waist and she lay her head on his chest, holding tight.

"I need to meet with our informant," he murmured, "but I should be back in forty-five minutes. No later than an hour. The others will stay with you until then."

She nodded and he pulled away. "Be safe."

He cupped his big, warm hand to her cheek. "Always."

***

The next morning Rane followed Jon into a conference room at the police station. When he'd arrived home last night he'd spent an hour deep in conversation with Denton before finally, blessedly, the house had been cleared of pissed-off, alpha males.

Jon had been preoccupied when he'd led her to bed, but once their clothes lay on the floor, he tossed her on the bed, and was on her like a starving man and she was the buffet. Their lovemaking held an intensity that while thrilling, made her anxious. She thought the pseudo kidnapping had rattled Jon, and he was working out his fears by taking as much as he could from her, while giving everything he had to make sure she knew how he felt.

He was probably psyching himself up for the end game, and that scared her. But when she'd woken up that morning with her head on his shoulder, his strong arm holding her close to his side, she had a feeling of security and contentment. It felt so right, *he* felt so right. She was tumbling into love with a man who, judging from his all-in personality, would have expectations of a commitment she couldn't fulfill.

Knowing what could be broke her heart.

Emotions on edge—she used to be comfortable in police stations, not anymore—she surveyed the assembled men before taking a seat. She and Jon both carried travel mugs. He'd insisted on taking the time to make coffee, saying he didn't want to poison her with the station's notorious brew. The entire team was present. Denton and Ben's heads were bent in conversation. Ty leaned against a wall with his arms folded across his chest wearing a scowl. Nathan looked like the quintessential bad boy with his long-sleeve black t-shirt, scruffy beard, and fuck you attitude.

Jon took her hand as they stopped to talk to his brother. "You get cleared?"

Nathan glared. "For desk duty. Sons of bitches want me to ride a desk when this whole damn thing goes down. I'm appealing it." That explained the attitude.

"Good luck with that."

"I might have the luck. The lieutenant owes me."

Denton turned to address the group. "Listen up. Eddie came through for us. We checked out his tip and it's credible. The DiNardos are getting a substantial shipment of heroin tomorrow in the early morning. It's coming in on a rental truck and will be delivered to a warehouse on the south side. This is a big one. Their plan is to divide it at the warehouse and send it to stash houses where it'll be cut for distribution. We want to get it before it leaves the warehouse."

"We'll need more than our team for the take down," Nathan said.

"I'll arrange the additional resources and monitor the situation throughout the day and keep you all informed. As of now, you all have the rest of the day off. Relax. Get some sleep. We'll meet tomorrow at oh-five-hundred."

The phone rang and Ben caught it, spoke for a second and handed it to Denton.

"Yeah," Denton said, gaze turning to Nathan. "Good. I'll tell him."

He hung up. "You're cleared for full duty. Don't know how you did it, but you're cleared."

Nathan's grin turned smug. "Pick up the lieutenant's teenage daughter and take her home instead of bringing her in for drunk and disorderly and he'll owe you one too. Glad I'm not her dad."

***

Rane stood in her living room staring out the front window. Mrs. Kershaw walked by, hat flopping in the late morning sun with Honey Pumpkin in tow, this time in a matching fuchsia outfit. Across the street a woman pushed a baby carriage. Rane could see the baby's feet clad in tiny striped socks, poking out from under a blanket. It all seemed so normal, far removed from the dark world of heroin, drug deals, and stash houses. Denton had arranged for a guard to be placed on her father, and Lily was staying at her parents' house. Because Jon was occupied elsewhere, despite Denton having given him the afternoon off, Rane had a plainclothes officer assigned to her.

Jon and Nathan were meeting Simon. He hadn't told her, but she was positive that's why they disappeared together. After their morning conference with the task force Jon had gotten a call and pulled his brother into a huddle. He'd arranged for the guy assigned to her to take her home, and then Jon and Nathan disappeared.

She sipped at her tea, hoping it would calm her nerves. It hadn't worked yet. She felt restless and jittery. On top of being worried about Jon and Nathan, she knew she should tell Jon about her father's involvement in Kyle's prosecution. She had to be honest with him, but she kept holding back. Her father had always valued his service as a street cop and then as a detective, and he'd solved some big cases. While no cop would have a problem when one of their own did something like take the lieutenant's daughter home rather than arresting her, planting evidence to get a conviction crossed way over the line. Her dad's reputation would be ruined and every good thing he'd ever done would be overshadowed by that one incident of poor judgment. They'd probably have to reopen some of his cases to make sure he hadn't messed them up.

That he'd done it to protect her made it even worse, and the fact that she hadn't come forward when she found out made her equally responsible.

She set down her mug and grabbed her car keys. "C'mon Rick," she said to the officer sitting at her kitchen table with the Seattle Times, "I want to go visit my dad."

They drove the two miles to the facility. The tea hadn't calmed her nerves but taking action might. When she turned on the windshield wipers to deal with the light drizzle, she noticed the wiper blades had been replaced. She no longer had one wiper trailing a piece of rubber across the glass. Jon must've done it. She shook her head. She'd dealt with her own problems for so long she wasn't sure how to react when someone took some of the burden. Now she had an inkling what people meant when they talked about love. It *was* the little things that mattered.

She approached her father's room and saw the uniformed officer standing at the door. She left Rick chatting with him outside and entered the room, closing the door behind her.

Her dad sat in his easy chair in front of a window where he could see the sun breaking up the clouds. He stared out at the feeder where birds merrily scattered seed. He looked up when she came in. His dark hair had faded to gray and his eyes, the same sea green as hers, had lost their spark. "Those are house finches. The ones with the red on their chests."

"Sure are a lot of them."

"Every now and then we get a goldfinch. Not so many of them, but they're pretty."

It always amazed her that he could remember things like the species of bird outside his window, but some days forget she was his daughter.

Framed photos of the both of them together sat on his nightstand as a reminder. Rane took a seat near the window and looked at him. He'd lost weight. He'd once seemed so tall, strong, and invincible. Now he was a shell of his former self, his brain stealing him away, little by little. She swallowed past the lump in her throat. "How's it going, Dad?"

He turned his attention to her. "When am I getting out of this place? Is it time to go home?"

She took a steadying breath. "This is home now, Dad. The people here are good to you."

He looked at her with suddenly clear eyes. "But it's not home."

"No, but it's someplace where you're safe." She hoped to God she was telling the truth. The cops knew the DiNardos had someone inside the unit, and he'd insinuated as much that night at the supermarket. Targeting medical facilities for the access to drugs was part of their operation.

"Dad, you have to be careful what you talk about with the nurses or anyone who visits."

He rubbed a hand over his thinning hair. "Nurses? They bother me about a hundred times a day."

"They're doing their jobs. I don't want you talking to them about things you did when you were a cop. Okay? Don't mention any of the cases you worked on. To anyone." When his attention returned to the birds outside, she sighed. "Dad, are you listening? Do you understand? Don't talk about the DiNardos or any of the cases you worked on." The good days when he was "there," when he seemed almost normal, were getting crowded out by the not-so-good days.

"Hawk came yesterday. Swooped down and got one of the little finches. Bloody bastard. Circle of life."

Resigned, she rose to leave. She crossed to her father and gave him a kiss on his cheek. He began humming the melody from "Mr. Bojangles" as she walked out of the room.

Back home, her nervousness returned and she thought she'd start climbing the walls waiting to hear from Jon. She had to believe that he and Nathan could take care of themselves. She worried about her dad, and wondered if she'd gotten through to him. There was no telling what he understood. She could only hope that when all this was over and Simon DiNardo was in prison, his organization destroyed, what her father had done would remain a secret.

The roar of a motorcycle registered and from a window she saw a big black and chrome bike rolling up her driveway. Even with his head covered in a helmet she recognized Jon. He wore a leather jacket, blue jeans, and boots.

Rick walked to a window and looked out, then went back to the couch. He was the most laidback man she'd ever met. He'd spent the last hour stretched out and reading John Steinbeck while she'd prowled the house, unable to settle on anything.

Jon used his key and came in the kitchen door. Rick called from the living room. "Hey, man. Anything up?"

Jon replied, his gaze on her. "Nope. Gonna see if my girl wants to go out for a ride." His hair was ruffled from the helmet, his cheeks ruddy from the chilled air. He raised his brows in question.

"What happened?" she whispered. "You met with Simon, didn't you?"

His expression hardened. Keeping his voice down, he replied, "Yeah, we met. There's no deal. Denton doesn't know about Savannah, but we told him Simon wanted a meeting and he okayed it." He caught her look. "I know, I'll tell you about her later. I think Denton knows there's more to the meeting than what we told him, but he's willing to trust us. Denton wanted us to work him, to go along with whatever Simon wanted, play him. God, I wanted to take him down right then, but we need more evidence to be sure he goes down for a long time."

"What would make him think you'd let him off?"

"He said he'd give us the dirt on some of the big suppliers if we agreed not to pursue him or his family. I saw the way he looked at Nathan and it confirmed what he really wants—my brother dead. Nathan sliced his face. Simon wants the heat off so he can go after my brother without having to worry about the rest of the task force. If he got a deal he'd be free to plan and wait as long as it takes to get Nathan, and probably me, too. But he got a phone call and started acting jumpy. He said he couldn't trust us and walked away."

Jon shook his head like he was trying to shake off his mood. He took her hand, rubbed a finger over her knuckles. "We need to get away from here for a while. Clear our heads. What do you think? Up for a motorcycle ride? Great day for it."

He was right about the day. The morning clouds had disappeared, leaving a gorgeous afternoon in their wake. Chilly, but clear. Getting away from everything, even for a little while, sounded really, really good. "How about we take my car?"

"That defeats the purpose of going for a ride."

"What is the purpose?"

"If I have to explain it's obvious you've never ridden on a motorcycle."

"True. But I have treated plenty of patients in the ER who have. They usually have broken bones and road rash."

"Come with me. I guarantee you won't end up with broken bones or road rash. It'll get your mind off everything that's going on."

She glanced out the window at the big machine in her driveway, uncertain. "I didn't know you had a motorcycle."

"I don't. It's Nathan's. C'mon sweetheart, live a little."

She chewed her lip. He looked hot as hell in all that black leather, his laser blue eyes challenging her.

Giving in more to the temptation that was Jon than the motorcycle, she agreed. "There's nothing wrong with being cautious, but okay. I hope I don't regret it."

Chapter Thirteen

Jon accelerated down the driveway and onto the road with Rane's arms wrapped tightly around his waist. At his suggestion, she'd put on jeans and a heavy jacket, and he'd strapped a helmet onto her head. They picked up speed, and she couldn't stop the thrill that shot through her. It felt amazing. It was sexy holding onto Jon with the big machine surging under them, and there was the liberating feeling of flying along the road under the open sky with the wind whistling past.

He rode through the city, then followed the ship canal until he hit Puget Sound where he headed north. Every couple miles, she turned her head, taking in the scenery. She loved Washington. She loved the ever-changing weather, the geography of the Sound, the eclectic mix of cultures. Yeah, it rained a lot, but she figured that only made days like this one all the more glorious.

She held Jon more tightly and leaned into a curve. On a straight away he opened the throttle, and they raced by woods where the deciduous trees had taken on their autumn colors, standing out in stark contrast to the deep green pines. Crossing an old bridge, she spotted a tumbling river far below dotted with moss-covered boulders

Almost an hour later he slowed the bike and pulled into a parking lot on the outskirts of a small town. The sign on the building read Tilly's Diner, and judging by the number of cars and trucks, it was a popular place. She swung off the motorcycle and stretched her legs.

Jon took her helmet and secured it to the bike. "You good for an early dinner?"

"Sure."

With her hand in his, he led her to the diner. The small, casual sign of affection made her warm inside. "So, what do you think? Does riding a motorcycle do anything for you?"

"Oh yeah. Now I get why people are willing to risk the broken bones and road rash."

"Days like today are made for a ride."

He opened the door for her to precede him inside where they were quickly seated in a booth. Realizing she was hungrier than she'd thought, she perused the menu. The waitress, wearing a Washington State U sweatshirt, a nose ring, and pink hair took their order. She returned almost immediately with the hot tea Rane had requested, and coffee for Jon.

While they waited for their meal, Rane absently stirred honey into her tea. "Are you nervous about tomorrow?"

He shook his head. "We'll go over all that this evening. Right now I don't want to talk about it. This is breathing space to clear our heads."

"Okay. You're right. I was about to go crazy pacing around the house waiting for something to happen."

The waitress came alongside their table, her arms laden with food. They'd both ordered clam chowder, which was served in a huge scooped out bowl of crusty bread. When she put a basket of rolls made of the same crusty bread between them, Rane figured the meal was about perfect.

As he ripped a roll in half, Jon said, "Tell me something I don't know about Rane Smith."

She spread butter on her roll and thought about his question. "I have a secret fascination with steampunk."

His grin flashed. "I wouldn't have guessed that. Do you dress up in the gear, go to steampunk parties?"

"I've been to a few parties, but I don't really have the wardrobe. I read just about anything in the genre and, of course, watch the movies."

"Van Helsing was steampunk, right? I liked that one."

"Hugh Jackman? What's not to like?" She spooned up a mouthful of chowder. "Your turn. What's something I don't know about Jon David Garretson?"

He narrowed his eyes as he considered the question. "Hmm. I ran away when I was ten."

"Really? Why? Did you have a fight with your parents?"

"No. My best friend Trevor and I had read *My Side of the Mountain*. You know, the story of the kid who takes off for the wilds of the Catskill Mountains to live off the land. We thought we'd make a stab at doing the same in Olympic National Park."

"What happened?"

"My dad found us at the ferry terminal. We had our backpacks and all sorts of junk ten-year-olds think is important. Mostly comic books and candy bars."

"Were you in trouble?"

"Not really. Mom was pissed, but I think my dad got it. He promised me and Trevor a backpacking trip where we'd practice survival skills the next summer if I swore not to run away again. It worked out."

"Good dad."

"Yeah."

They lingered over the meal and by the time they left the diner the sun had almost completed its descent behind low mountains in the west, turning the sky the deepest blue. She climbed onto the motorcycle, put on her helmet, and held Jon tight when he accelerated and the bike picked up speed. Hurtling down the highway as night fell and stars began their arc across the sky was nothing short of magical. Rane hugged the feeling close as she tightened her arms around him and laid her cheek against his back, not wanting to let this memory slip away in the worry of what the coming days would bring.

***

Rane stared at Jon incredulously. "What do you mean, safe house? Why do I have to go to a safe house if you're here with me?"

"Because I don't trust DiNardo, and I have to leave early in the morning before sunrise. I want you someplace where I won't have to worry that piece of shit will grab you again."

Rane stared at Jon. She hated that he was right. Simon was unpredictable and if Jon was worrying about her, then his attention wasn't focused on the job. He'd been so relaxed earlier when they'd taken the motorcycle ride. *She'd* been so relaxed. Now reality was staring at them and it was time to face it. "Okay, fine. I'll go to a safe house. Where will you be?"

"Cooper and I will be here in case DiNardo tries something."

She'd loved being with Jon at night, and the thought of him not being near gave her an unsettled feeling. She wanted to believe it was because he made her feel safe, but she was kidding herself if she thought her feelings went no deeper than that. Aware of how well he could read her, she forced herself to address the issue at hand. "I'd better pack an overnight bag, then."

Jon followed her up the stairs to her room. She pulled a duffle bag from her closet and began gathering enough clothing to get her through the next day. Aware of his sharp blue gaze following her every move she pulled out underwear from her dresser drawer.

He moved to peek over her shoulder. Reaching in a finger, he snagged silky lace panties in emerald green. "Hmm. I like these."

"Yeah? Maybe I'll let you borrow them sometime."

"Not exactly what I had in mind."

"Right." She looked over her shoulder to see his expression turn serious.

He reached up to brush his fingers lightly along her temple. "It'll be all right, sweetheart. We'll get through this, and then you and I can talk about our future."

She ducked her head and pulled practical cotton underwear and a bra from the drawer. She sucked in a breath and the words followed in a rush. "Jon, I don't want you to get the wrong idea. I—"

His arm dropped around her shoulders and he turned her to face him. "Shh. It's okay. We'll talk later when we don't have so much hanging over our heads." He brushed a kiss across her lips.

Rane nodded. She really didn't want to have that conversation now anyway. "Okay. But can you tell me about Savannah? What's her connection with you and Simon?"

She saw his hesitation. He stepped back and paced toward the window where he parted the blind to look out into the dark night before turning back toward her. "I'll tell you, but the team doesn't know about this."

She nodded and he began to speak. "Savannah was Nathan's girlfriend. He'd met her in college. She was younger than him by a few years. He'd worked for a while before going to the university, and she'd begun right out of high school. She was incredibly bright, a straight A student involved in all kinds of community projects. Her home life was a mess so I think she threw herself into school and outside activities to get away from it."

He paused, spearing a hand through his hair, moving restlessly around the room before continuing. "I'd gotten out of basic and had come home for a visit before deploying when I met her for the first time. She was so pretty and full of life. I was happy for Nate. I don't think he'd ever really been in love before, but I could tell she was it for him."

He stopped his restless movements and stood with his hands jammed in his pockets. Rane thought he wasn't seeing her or the room, he was caught in the memories of an earlier time. "I started noticing that something was off. Little things. Like how she was so organized and seemed to have her act together, and then she'd go missing for a day. We'd made plans to meet at the ferry and go across to Bainbridge Island, and she didn't show. Said she'd gotten sick and hadn't been able to call."

When he paused, she prompted him. "But she wasn't sick?"

He shook his head. "Nathan bought it. He bought anything she told him. But I'd seen the same kind of thing in a guy I'd gone to basic with. That guy washed out because of a drug habit he couldn't kick."

Rane thought she knew where the story was heading. "She was hooked on drugs."

"Yeah, she was. I tried to tell Nathan but he wouldn't hear it. Talk about being blinded by love."

Expression grim, he went on. "It wasn't only Nathan. Savannah didn't see it. She thought if she was a model student, had a boyfriend, volunteered her time to help the needy, she couldn't be an addict, a junkie."

"She told you this?"

"Yeah. I was really worried. I was shipping out in a few days and I'd tried to talk to Nate. Got a fist to the face for my trouble. Ninety percent of the time, that's his default when he's pissed. He wouldn't see it so I decided I had to talk to her. Get her to come clean so she could get some help. But she denied it. I think she could have passed a lie detector test because she'd walled off that part of her life, completely separate from the front she showed Nathan and the rest of the world."

"You had to leave, to go to Afghanistan?"

"Yeah. I had to go. The next time I had leave I was only home for a couple days, and honestly, I couldn't tell if she was still using.

Maybe I was fooling myself because I wanted Nathan to be happy. They were both set to graduate in a couple months and I know my brother planned to propose. I wanted it to be right for them and I fooled myself into believing it was."

He began prowling the room again and, Rane pulled open a dresser drawer to grab a pair of jeans.

"Then she died."

She stood clutching the jeans to her chest. "Overdose?"

"Yeah. Nathan found her in her apartment. She'd been injecting heroin between her toes so no one would notice the needle marks. She got some bad dope and ended up dead."

Rane's heart ached for what was lost. A beautiful young woman, a young man's world. She saw the pain in Jon's eyes and thought she understood. "It's not your fault. You tried to warn them."

"I know it's not my fault, but I still wish I'd done something to stop it. I saw the train wreck coming and I left for the other side of the world and let it happen."

"People make their own choices. Even if you'd stayed, it doesn't mean you could've stopped it. The only person who could've stopped it was Savannah, and she paid with her life."

"Yeah, she did."

Something clicked in Rane's brain, something that made the whole picture clearer. "Ah. Simon was her dealer."

"No." He looked at her, his expression enigmatic. "Kyle was."

Her mind reeled. Kyle had supplied the heroin that had killed Savannah. She took a guess at the outcome. "Nathan went after Kyle?"

"Initially. He found Kyle, beat the crap out of him. The next thing Nathan knew, a couple thugs showed up at his door and he ended up in the hospital. After that, he decided to play it smart. He realized Kyle was low level. He did some digging and found out Kyle's brother was the brains. Simon was and is the drug kingpin supplying most of Seattle with heroin."

"That's when Nathan decided to go after Simon."

"I said he got smart. He went to the police academy, joined the force and learned everything he could about the illegal narcotics trade."

"Wow. That's patience. He's waited a long time to get to Simon."

Jon shook his head. "Not so long. About a year after he got out of the academy he volunteered for a raid on a stash house. It went sideways. They hadn't expected Simon to be there, and if he's there, extra protection is there. The upshot was an officer got shot. Nathan lost his gun in the chaos. He ended up alone in the kitchen with Simon and two of his goons and no gun. All he had was a pocketknife. He managed to take a slice out of Simon's face before he was thrown into a wall and fractured his wrist. They would've killed him if backup hadn't rushed the place right then. Simon slipped away, like he always does."

Rane sat on the bed as she thought through the implications. "You said the team doesn't know about Savannah, about you and Nathan's connection to the DiNardos."

"No, they don't know. We'd never have gotten on the task force if they'd known."

"You joined the police department when you got out of the army for the same reason as Nathan? To take down the DiNardos?" Her voice sounded calm, but she didn't feel calm. Her stomach churned and she suddenly felt nauseous.

"Only partly. I joined for people like Savannah, victims of shitheads like Simon who make a living off of ruining people's lives. Off of death."

"Why couldn't you tell me this before when I found out you were a cop and had rented my apartment to spy on me?"

She watched his expression harden. "You didn't need to know."

"Really? I didn't need to know when I was acting as a double agent? You don't think I needed to be armed with as much information as possible when Simon had me in his car, driving me around the city so he could explain how easily he could murder me or my father?"

"That's exactly why you didn't need to know. You acted surprised when Simon brought up Savannah, right? You're safer if Simon thinks you aren't so close that I'd tell you everything. He's already after you because of your connection to Kyle. You'd be an even bigger prize if he thought you and I were involved to the point that I'd tell you about Savannah, something Nathan and I have kept quiet about. He's got to know we haven't been up front with the task force. That we'd be booted to the side because of our conflict of interest if they found out."

Angry, Rane's words came out heated. "I think you should have told me about that. I'm the one playing both sides. The more information I had the better prepared I'd be. You should have trusted me."

"This isn't about trust. It's about shutting down the DiNardos and sending every damned one of them to prison."

"Getting close to me, sleeping with me, someone who has a connection with them, was a good way to achieve your ultimate goal, revenge for Savannah's death."

"Justice is different than revenge. You *know* I'm not using you. It may've started out with me going undercover to rent the apartment from you, but things changed. You know they did. I didn't plan on getting into a relationship."

"So that opportunity was too good to pass up." She couldn't help feeling hurt that he hadn't been completely honest, but had to admit she was equally guilty. She hadn't told Jon what her father had done, and by now, she should have.

He crossed the room to stand in front of her, tension evident in the set of his shoulders. "It wasn't like that. You know it. You twisted me up. We're together because we can't not be together."

Rane pushed off the bed. She jerked open the closet door and grabbed her boots. "That makes a lot of sense," she muttered.

"I didn't say it makes sense. You've got nothing to be pissed about. I've been as honest as I could, given the circumstances. You might have tried the same."

"What's that supposed to mean?"

"Exactly what I said. You didn't tell me about your dad, about his connection to Kyle."

She stopped arranging clothes in the duffel, wary. "What connection?"

His expression remained grim. "Still trying to play it close, huh? When you and Kyle met, you talked about a connection between his prosecution and your dad. Want to explain what that was about?"

"Dad was a cop, so sure, he may have been involved in Kyle's arrest. Other cops were, too."

He was silent for a long moment and with a sinking feeling, she guessed he knew she was lying. Voice quiet, she tried again. "You're grabbing at straws."

"Your dad planted the heroin that sent Kyle to prison."

"How do you know? Did Simon say something?" She narrowed her eyes in speculation. "It wasn't Simon, was it? It was Kyle. How do you know what we talked about? Kyle said something when we met that day at the hospital. The two cops you had at the tables weren't close enough to hear us." She paused, thinking hard. "You wanted to put a wire on me but I'd refused." Realization dawned. "You wired me anyway, didn't you? You somehow snuck a wire on me."

He jammed his fingers through his hair, making it stand on end. "Okay. Yeah, I put a bug in the strap of your lunch box."

Rane walked up to him and drilled a finger into his chest. "After I refused to wear a wire, and you agreed I didn't have to. Another lie."

He grabbed her hand and held tight when she would have jerked away. "I never agreed. I stopped arguing about it, that's all."

"You distracted me with shower sex so I wouldn't notice you hadn't agreed."

"No. *You* distracted *me* with shower sex. God, Rane. You make me so crazy I can't think half the time."

Tension arced between them, and she tried to keep herself in check. She'd let herself get lured into the idea that she could, possibly, maybe, end up with him. She had to remember that their relationship had started with deception, and as far as she was concerned, trust and honesty were rare commodities. She pulled back and this time he let go of her hand. "This never would have gone anywhere anyway. It's good we got this out in the open now."

"What the hell do you mean by that? We're not done."

"Yeah, we are. I don't do relationships, and you've proven why. People lie, they can't be trusted."

"That's crap. Nothing in life is black and white. Yeah, I didn't tell you about Savannah because it wasn't my story to tell, and I thought you would be safer not knowing. Denton ordered you had to be wired when you met with Kyle."

"Sounds convenient."

"It's the truth. They may be in the gray zone, but my reasons were sound. I'm betting your reasons for holding back about your dad aren't exactly black and white either."

Shoulders slumped, Rane looked around the room as if the walls would have answers. "It doesn't matter anymore."

She grabbed the duffel and walked out of the room.

Chapter Fourteen

Jon checked his Glock and secured it in his holster, he had to focus on the coming operation. Rane was taken care of. He'd gotten her to the safe house and despite his opposition, Denton had assigned Ty to guard her. Jon didn't hundred percent trust the guy. There was something he couldn't put his finger on. Ty irritated Jon most of the time, but he didn't have anything solid against him, so he'd given in when Denton had held firm. Ty had pulled a hamstring earlier in the week so he couldn't be in on the raid, but he could watch Rane in the safe house.

Jon followed Ben and Nathan into the van and with Denton driving, passed through the quiet streets in the early morning dark. They reached their destination and parked in an alley about a block from the warehouse and quickly exited the vehicle. Like the backup team who had followed in a van behind them, he moved silently through the darkness to take up his position. The air felt heavy with moisture brought in by fog rolling in off the ocean. He slipped on his earpiece and heard Nathan confirm to Denton that he was in place. "I'm good," he said into his mic.

The team waited on the perimeter of the warehouse until, as Eddie had claimed would happen, a rental truck pulled up and began backing into a loading bay. Following the plan, Nathan crept up behind the driver as he stepped out of the truck, phone in his hand glowing.

"Hey, dude, you got a light?" The man whirled to find Nathan, dressed like a bum, a cigarette dangling from his lips.

Using the diversion, Jon ran around the back of the truck.

"Where'd you come from?"

From Jon's vantage point, he could see the driver looking around nervously.

Nathan shuffled closer. "I been sleepin' in that empty building over there." He waved a hand to his left and when the driver followed the movement, Nathan raised a fist and clipped him on the chin. The guy crumpled like a puppet with its strings cut. Jon got the guy's cell and kept the screen from darkening even as they pulled the driver around the building where he was taken by two team members to be cuffed and placed in the van.

Jon examined the phone and found recent texts. He punched in a message.

Shipments here.

A response came almost immediately.

Wait there. Will open loading door.

He and Nathan flanked the loading bay door. The teams took up position and when the door slid up, they swarmed in. In a matter of minutes and without a shot being fired, it was over. DiNardo's men were cuffed and taken to a holding area for transport.

Denton motioned Jon over to the rear of the rental truck and pushed up the rolling door. The back was full of pallets stacked with crates. They got a crowbar and Jon pried the top off one. Inside were bags marked as Colombia's finest roast coffee beans. He took out a pen knife and slit open a bag. Dark beans spilled onto the floor. The smell made him wish for a cup, strong and black, but coffee beans weren't what he was looking for. He slit open another bag, and, stomach sinking, another. More coffee beans. Fuck. Denton grabbed a bag and used his knife. Again, just coffee. The rest of the team joined them and they went through all the bags. Coffee. No heroin. Only coffee.

Jon stalked out of the truck, Nathan following. They walked out into the parking lot, now swarming with police cars. "Son of a bitch. What the hell happened? I could have sworn Eddie was telling us straight."

"Yeah, Eddie was being straight." His narrowed his eyes. "They were onto us. They knew we were coming. That's the only explanation."

"Shit. The whole operation's shot to hell. This was supposed to give us what we needed to put them away." Jon felt like his head was buzzing as he sorted through the ramifications of the failed raid. "We've got to have Eddie picked up. If the DiNardos figure out he's our source, they'll go after him. Whatever went wrong, it wasn't his fault."

"Yeah, you're right. Tell Denton."

Jon raised his brows at the distracted tone but crossed the parking lot to talk to the team leader.

"I'll have Eddie picked up." Denton spoke with his usual unflappable calm.

Both men looked up when Nathan approached. "It's Ty," he growled.

"What?" Denton's tone sharpened.

"It's got to be Ty. He's the leak." Barely controlled rage underlined Nathan's tone. "They were ready for us. They've been one move ahead of the team every step of the way. That raid where I got shot? They knew we were hitting that stash house and had fucking ARs. Remember Ty wasn't along on that raid? Bailed for some reason. They knew we were coming here." He looked at Jon. "We've got to get to Rane."

Jon felt an icy ball of fear lodge in his gut as the truth sank in. At Denton's okay, the brothers commandeered a patrol car, and with Nathan behind the wheel, they raced through the city toward the safe house, siren wailing, lights flashing. Tires squealed as they reached the white stucco house on the tree-lined street. Jon had his door open and was running up the walkway before Nathan had fully stopped the vehicle. The front door was locked and he pounded, waited, and then pounded again. Nathan joined him and at his brother's nod, they both stepped back and kicked, sending the door crashing in.

Ty lay slumped on the floor. He raised himself groggily to his knees, a goose egg prominent on his forehead.

"Rane!" Jon ran through the kitchen and then down a back hall, flipping on lights as he went. He found the room she'd slept in. Her purse sat on the nightstand, the flannel pants he remembered her packing lying on the bed. A quick search of the rest of the house showed the back door broken in, and confirmed the nightmare was real. She was gone.

He returned to the front of the house. Nathan had Ty on his feet, back against the wall, an arm across his throat. "Where is she, you fucking piece of shit?"

"I don't know." Eyes wild, Ty's voice sounded panicked as he struggled to breathe. "They knocked me out, man. I came to when you guys kicked in the door." When Nathan pressed harder on his neck, Ty's eyes wheeled in his head. "Jon. Call him off."

Jon grabbed the front of Ty's shirt as Denton charged into the room behind them. Nathan loosened his hold as Jon yanked Ty close until they were nose to nose. "Where'd they take her? Anything happens to her there's not a hole deep enough for you to crawl in that I won't find you."

He shook off Denton's restraining grip but lost his hold when he found himself being hauled back by the back of his jacket, Denton's face an inch from his. "Stand down. If he's the leak, we'll take care of it. But we'll do it right. You and Nathan back off."

Nathan grabbed Jon's arm to keep him from going after Ty again as the man started babbling excuses. Jon shook free and strode back to the bedroom. This time he went in carefully, scanning for anything that would point to where Rane had been taken. He dumped the contents of her purse and cursed silently when he saw her phone. No chance of tracking her that way. The suitcase she'd packed for the night didn't yield any clues, nor did a search of the rest of the house. He returned to the living room where Ty was being escorted out, hands cuffed behind his back.

Everyone turned toward him.

"The bastard's taken her and she doesn't have her cell on her."

***

Rane held herself stiffly against the movement of the vehicle. With a dark hood pulled over her head she'd lost all sense of direction. Initially, she'd tried to make a mental map of where they were going based on the turns and distance on straightaways, but it had become impossible. She swallowed convulsively to force down the nausea brought by motion sickness and fear. Her stomach pitched as they rounded a turn and then, blessedly, the vehicle stopped.

They hadn't been driving for that long and she suspected they were still in the city. The safe house, well, the *not so safe* house, had been near downtown and she guessed they'd only driven maybe fifteen to twenty minutes. Focusing on details, on things that might help her survive, helped push back on the abject terror that had filled her when she'd seen Ty.

She'd woken early and taken a quick shower. A commotion had brought her from the bedroom, and when she reached the front of the house she'd found his still form prone on the floor. She'd bent over him and that's when they'd gotten her.

She was grabbed from behind, a hood pulled over her head. She'd fought, struggling wildly, even breaking away at one point. She'd pulled off the hood and, in the scramble that followed, kicked, punched, and clawed at Mick. The other guy she'd never seen before. He grabbed her around the waist and Mick planted a fist in her face that snapped her head back and bloodied her lip. She hadn't stood a chance. Covering her head, they shoved her into what had to be the cargo space of a van, hands bound behind her. Kyle had been right. Simon DiNardo was moving ahead with his plan to kill her.

She had to think past the fear. She braced herself when the back of the van opened and rough hands pulled her out. She stumbled and was yanked to her feet. The hood was jerked off her head and she smelled the tang of the ocean and heard the knocking sounds of boats pulling against their moorings.

"Get moving." The order was accompanied by a rough push.

The light of daybreak was muted by thick fog, giving everything a monochromatic look of black and gray. The two men gripped her arms and forced her to walk in front of them.

They passed between cavernous buildings she thought might have once been canneries. The raucous cries of gulls blended with the barking of seals and the chugging of an engine, all muted by the damp air. She tried to see as much as she could, trying to absorb details that might be useful to help her escape. She *had* to escape.

They approached a dock where the masts of sailing vessels and commercial fishing ships speared into the fog. Fishing boats meant fishermen, she hoped. She drew in a deep breath to steady her nerves and smelled the slightly rotting odor she associated with Seattle's wharves. Where were the fishermen? She would've thought the place would be full of activity, but maybe fishermen took Sunday off.

Her captors changed direction and the docks disappeared from view as they moved between two buildings.

"We've got to get her inside before we're seen." This came from Mick.

"Do you think the boss will kill her?" The second man's voice sounded uncertain.

"He'll do whatever he does. You're an asshole, Juan. Don't start with the cold feet now."

"I don't have cold feet. I don't want to be there when he kills her, that's all. I know he's your cousin but the boss gives me the creeps, man."

"Shut up, you idiot."

She'd been trying to keep her head, to be smart, think about her surroundings, to look for the best avenue of escape. Now, Rane felt terror seep deep into her bones, settling over her like a frozen black curtain that sapped her resolve and blocked out any possibility of escape. Not paying attention in the half light, she stumbled and found herself caught against Juan's slightly pudgy body that stank of sweat and body odor. "Hey, I think she likes me."

Rane instantly tried to pull away but his grip tightened on her elbow. Mick unlocked the warehouse door, and Juan pushed her up a short flight of steps.

The harbor sounds faded as they entered a building. They crossed an open space where a moving van was parked, its rolling back door up to expose an empty cargo space. Its engine emitted the quiet ticking sounds of a vehicle recently driven. They stopped at a door along the far wall, open to a lighted office. A burly man with short-cropped dark hair sat at a desk littered with Coke cans. The air reeked of stale cigarette smoke.

Mick motioned Juan to stay with Rane in the doorway while he entered the room and asked, "You get the product moved?"

"What do you think? Do I look like a moron?"

"Answer the fucking question, Pete. Did you get the dope out of the van and onto the boat?" Mick sounded like he was barely holding onto his temper.

"Boss told me to move it, so I moved it." The man at the desk rubbed his hands gleefully. "I wish I could have seen the faces on those cops when they got the dummy van and figured out there was no dope, only coffee beans. Stupid assholes."

"Shut it, dumbass. You're coming with me. We've got to get the van out, and get this place ready to blow." He turned to Juan. "Lock her in the workroom and then come out back," Mick snapped out the command then walked down the hall with Pete.

Juan pulled Rane toward a door further along the same wall. The outline of a plan was taking shape in her head. Figuring Juan as the weak link, she deliberately tripped again, this time almost falling to her knees. When he pulled her to her feet, she let out a tremulous sigh and, fighting the urge to gag, affected a breathy voice. "Thank you."

He responded with a brief grunt but she could see his gaze slide over her face, her breasts. He unlocked the door and stuck the keys in his pocket. Standing with his back to the door to hold it open, he waited for her to enter the pitch black room.

"I have to go in there?" It wasn't much of a stretch to make her voice quaver with anxiety. It was really dark. "Is it okay to turn on a light?"

"No light."

"Well, could you at least untie my hands? I can't be in there in the dark with my hands tied. There might be rats. Or cockroaches." She added hesitantly, "Please?"

She could tell he was wavering. "I'll turn on the light but that's it. You stay tied."

He flipped the switch and a naked bulb suspended from the ceiling glowed dimly. Rane crossed the threshold, stepping carefully around a jumbled pile of what looked like metal tools and chains. A couch, stuffing coming out of the cushions and sagging at one end, sat along a far wall, and a work bench littered with beer and soda cans ran across another. She turned to look over her shoulder. "Do you think—"

Juan stepped back, eyes downcast, and slammed the door shut.

***

Jon crouched beside the SWAT van, waiting for the signal to go. The DiNardo compound looked vacant. Through the tall pines he studied the large two-story house that sat on a hill with outbuildings spread below. Security appeared tighter than around a prison. They'd cut the electricity about five minutes ago and immediately heard the backup generators as they kicked on. A low rumble sounded through the damp air and he turned to see the police department's armored vehicle making its way up the driveway. As it neared the locked gate, the only section of the perimeter without electric barbed wire, it maintained its speed and crashed through, flattening the gate and pulling down the surrounding fence.

At the signal from the SWAT leader, the team followed the vehicle over the downed gate, avoiding the wire they assumed was still charged by the generators. They'd expected a firefight, but there were no gunshots, no flurry of activity. Jon had the sinking feeling the place was abandoned.

If that was true, Rane wasn't here and there was no predicting where she'd been taken.

The outbuildings were quickly searched. There were no cars or trucks, which confirmed that the DiNardos had taken off.

The SWAT team lobbed cameras attached to remote controlled vehicles through windows in the house in both the upstairs and the downstairs. Jon took a seat in the van watching the display screens as two officers used hand-held controls to send the little robots scurrying around the house. The images showed empty room after empty room. There was no sign that anyone had even lived there recently. There were no dirty clothes on the floor or dishes on a counter. The entire place was too neat.

Jon sighed impatiently. "We might as well go in and check it out ourselves, make sure no one's hiding in a closet, and then we can move on to our next target."

One of the guys with a remote control gave him a quick look. "Where's the next target?"

"No idea. But once we know for sure she's not here, then we can start figuring that out."

"Looks clear so far."

"Wait." This came from the guy with the other remote, the one that operated the downstairs robot. "Look at that." He enlarged the screen to show a thin wire snaking from the bottom of the front door to a metal toolbox. "Gentlemen, I'd say that place is rigged to blow. This will take some time."

While they waited for a bomb disposal robot to do its job, Jon and Nathan met with the rest of the team behind the SWAT vehicle. If Jon didn't find Rane, if he didn't have some assurance soon that she was safe, he'd lose his mind.

Worry gnawed at his gut and he kept playing that last scene with her through his mind. They'd argued about him placing the bug on her. She'd been angry he hadn't told her about Savannah. Their last real conversation had been an argument, and what he'd really wanted to say to her, what had been skirting around the edges of his brain for the past week, was that he was in love with her. He'd managed to avoid any emotional entanglements his entire adult life, and yet, he'd fallen fast and hard.

He shook his head to clear it. He had to focus, to keep the anxiety dialed back and under control. He'd be no use helping to find her if he couldn't stay centered and think rationally. "She's not here. We've got to make a new plan."

Denton nodded his head and spoke in his gravelly voice. "We'll go back to the station, do some digging. We need to find out what other properties these bastards might own or use where they could have taken her."

Jon nodded his agreement because he didn't have any other ideas. It didn't feel right. He didn't think Simon was "holding" Rane. From her conversation with Kyle, Jon knew Simon planned to kill her.

But first he'd use her as to get at him and Nathan.

"The old man, you think he knows more than we do?"

Jon looked at his brother. "What do you mean?"

Nathan stood, hands in his pockets. He'd ditched the ragged clothing and ratty ball cap he'd used to play the bum. "Doug Smith. I know his mind's shot, but sometimes those folks can have lucid moments. It's been years since he was involved in that case, but I wonder if he'd have any idea where they've taken her."

Willing to try anything, Jon cocked a brow at Denton, who nodded. "You two go over to his facility, see if you can get anything out of him. Ben and I'll go back to headquarters."

Nathan snagged the keys to the squad car and Jon hit the siren as they raced to talk to a man whose memories were mostly lost to him.

Chapter Fifteen

Jon showed his badge at the front desk of the memory care wing of the assisted living facility, and was led to a room where a uniform officer kept watch at the door. Douglas Smith sat in a chair by the window, staring out at birds rioting around a loaded feeder. Jon bet Rane kept it full for her dad.

"Mr. Smith, do you mind if we have a word."

The old man turned his head to look at him. "Who are you?"

Age and disease had sapped the man's vitality. Jon couldn't imagine how Rane dealt with losing a piece of her father every day. He cleared his throat. "I'm Detective Jon Garretson, Seattle PD. I'm hoping you can help me with an old case."

He thought he saw a spark of interest in the faded eyes. "What case?"

"The DiNardo case." This time the change in his expression was definite and Jon knew he remembered.

"My daughter doesn't want me to talk about it."

"Sir, this is important. Rane would be okay with us talking." He didn't want to bring up Rane's disappearance and agitate the man. Jon needed Doug to focus.

"Bastard got what he deserved. Should've never let him get within ten feet of my little girl."

Jon couldn't fault him for that sentiment. "I'm not so interested in Kyle DiNardo. I need to know anything you remember about Simon and his organization."

"Bad business that one. Something not right up here." He tapped his temple and Jon found himself nodding in agreement.

"You're right. I need to find him before he hurts someone."

Smith turned back to stare at the birds.

"Sir," Jon paused when he got no response. "Mr. Smith, do you remember any property the DiNardos own besides their compound? Anywhere they'd go if they wanted to lay low for a while?"

When a dull gaze returned to his, Jon wondered if he'd lost Smith, if whatever moment of clarity he'd had was gone. Doug took a shaky breath and muttered, "He was running dope up the coast."

"Did he have a warehouse?"

"Heaven's Bounty."

"What? What's Heaven's Bounty?"

Smith's gaze went again to the birds taking turns alighting on the feeder. "That one little bugger keeps chasing the others off. Thinks all that seed's his."

"Mr. Smith, what's Heaven's Bounty?"

The old man shook his head and stared out the window, humming a tune under his breath Jon recognized as "Mr. Bojangles."

***

Rane continued her fumbling search of the dimly lit room. She'd lost track of time, but figured she must have been in the room for at least an hour, maybe longer. She'd been looking for something with a rough edge she could use to cut through the zip ties that bound her wrists. Having her hands behind her back made movement incredibly awkward and slow. The hard plastic bindings hurt where they bit into her skin. She'd tried a rough piece of metal, had worked at it for quite a while, and had ended up with scraped wrists and not much else.

She used her foot to shift the haphazard pile of tools on the floor. Nothing promising there. She moved farther along the wall, and then spied something that raised her hopes. A handle lay under a greasy cloth, the same shape as a tool her father had once owned. Turning around she reached back with her bound hands, grasped the handle, and pulled it free. A hacksaw, its blade splotchy with rust. Heart pounding, she looked around for someplace she could wedge it where it would be held firm so she could get it between her wrists and work at the plastic bindings. With her hands free, she had a chance.

Inspiration struck and she took it to the couch. She sat on the handle to hold it steady, angled her arms awkwardly, and began rubbing the binding against the blade. Even with the blade cutting into her skin, she kept up the movement, giving a quick thanks that her tetanus shot was up to date.

The zip tie finally gave and, muscles aching, she brought her hands to her front. She was surprised she was being held in a room with such obvious tools to help her get free. Her captors either thought she was too stupid to try, or didn't think she'd get far if she did free her hands. Using her shirt to wipe at the blood smeared on her wrists, she paused, straining to hear.

The sound of raised voices carried through the wall, muffled and nearly indistinguishable. Someone was seriously unhappy, his voice harsh and threatening. It was hard to make out more than a few words. She did catch "overboard" and a string of profanity, and then, quite distinctly, "Do this, or the same will happen to you. Got it?"

Whoever responded must have gotten it because the speaker said, "Good," and then the voices quieted. She moved to press her ear to the door, listening intently, barely breathing. Two sets of footsteps echoed down the corridor outside the room. She chewed her lip. Who did that leave in the office? Maybe the two sets of footsteps had been Mick and Pete, the guy who'd been in the office when they'd arrived. If she was lucky, Juan had once again been left alone. Now might be her chance.

Quickly returning the saw to the workbench, she grabbed the zip tie and shoved it under the couch. She pulled down the sleeves of her jacket before moving back to the door. She tried the doorknob on the remote chance it wasn't locked. It didn't budge so she gave a soft kick. When that got no response, she kicked again, a little harder, this time calling out, "Hello, can anyone hear me?"

Waiting, ears pricked, she finally heard a shuffling noise through the door, something being pushed aside and the jingle of keys. She stepped back, whipping her hands behind her back. The door opened and relief washed through her when Juan stuck his head in. "What do you want?"

She kept her voice low and soft, trying to sound as non-threatening as possible. "Please, I need to use the bathroom." When he stared at her, she injected a pleading tone into voice. "I really have to go."

He glanced furtively up and down the hall then backed up a step. "There's a bathroom in there." He jerked his head toward the office. "Be quick."

She'd have to make plans as she went, but this could be her only chance. With her hands clasped behind her and fervently hoping he wouldn't notice that her hands weren't really bound, she preceded him out of the room and down the hall. He motioned her into the office. She stepped in and saw something that made her heart jump. A phone. Someone had left their phone plugged into a charger on the desk.

"Juan. Get over here." The call came from down the hall and Juan turned his head to respond. "Yeah, I'm coming."

He looked back and Rane turned to face him, hands behind her back as she edged toward the bathroom door. "I'll only be a minute."

She backed into the bathroom and quickly shut the door. The room smelled like it hadn't been cleaned in years, which was probably why the tiny window high on the wall above the toilet was open to the outside. She brought her hands in front of her, gripping her prize tightly. In that moment when Juan had turned his attention away she had grabbed the phone off the desk. Hoping against hope that he wouldn't notice the empty charger, she pressed the on button. The phone was password protected but she tapped the emergency call button at the bottom of the screen and, fingers flying, keyed in a number.

The phone was ringing in her ear when a sharp knock sounded at the door. "Get done in there."

"I'm working on it, really," she replied. "It's hard with my hands behind my back."

She heard a grunt in return. The phone picked up and she flushed the toilet to hide her voice.

"Garretson."

"Jon." The sound of his voice almost undid her. She squeezed her eyes shut to force back the tears suddenly welling up. Being terrified wasn't an excuse to fall apart.

"Rane, sweetheart, where are you?"

She stepped onto the toilet seat to look out the window. Making her voice as low as possible and still be heard, she said, "I'm at a warehouse down at the docks. Two guys got me. They work for Simon."

"Baby, can you give me any more than that?"

"They're big warehouses that might've been canneries. But I think they're moving me to a boat." Her voice wavered. "They're planning to kill me. I think they're going to take me out on the boat and throw me overboard. Then they'll try to get you and Nathan too, somehow."

"Sweetheart, don't worry about us. We'll find you."

The door rattled and she called out, "I'm almost done. I'll be out in a sec." She turned on the faucet, sending a blast of water into the stained sink. "I've got to go."

"Rane, wait. Don't disconnect. Keep the connection as long as you can so we can use it to pinpoint your location."

"Okay," she whispered. "I'll see what I can do."

In the end, she stuck the phone up her jacket sleeve with the screen facing away from her arm so her body heat wouldn't accidently disconnect them. The jacket was bulky enough, and with her hands behind her back, she thought Juan might not notice.

Talking with Jon, hearing the steady tone of his voice, however briefly, gave her hope that maybe she could survive this. With her hands behind her back she opened the door to find Juan with his fist raised to pound once again. "C'mon, before they come back. They'll work me over if they know I let you out." He grabbed her elbow to propel her out of the office.

Her stomach sank when two men came toward them down the hall.

"What the fuck? What'd you let her out for?" Mick snarled.

"She needed to pee. What was I supposed to do?"

Mick swore ripely and stalked into the office while the other man stopped in front of them. Rane's blood froze as she looked into the ghostly pale eyes of Simon DiNardo.

"Rane, I see you've joined us." He smiled his lipless smile, causing the scar along the side of his face to pucker. "As you can tell, we've moved on to the next stage of our plan." She couldn't suppress a shudder. The man was so cold, so unfeeling, all the humanity had leached out of him to leave a shell of undiluted evil.

"Son of a bitch, where the fuck's my phone?"

Simon's eyes never left hers when Mick surged back into the hall. Juan stepped back hastily as Mick jerked Rane by the shoulder. Rough hands felt her pockets, then around her waist band. She kept her hands clasped tightly behind her, fear causing her blood to thunder in her ears. Her heart dropped when Mick let out a hissing breath. Grasping her wrist, he yanked her hands apart, jerking one hand in front of her and turning to glare at Juan.

"You asshole. Her hands aren't even tied."

Rane felt a flash of sympathy for Juan. Mick continued his search, making her stomach turn when he ran a thumb under the cup of her bra. She held her breath, fingers tightening around the cuff of her jacket sleeve to keep the phone from slipping out, but then he brushed his arm against it. "Fuck." He stuck his fingers under the cuff and pulled it free.

Without missing a beat, he pivoted and sucker punched Juan, snapping the man's head back with a blow to the jaw that sent him sprawling across the floor. Rane bit her lip to keep from crying out. She didn't want to feel compassion for Juan. He may have let her use the bathroom, but he'd still taken part in kidnapping her.

Simon held out his hand and Mick gave him the phone. He looked at the screen and raised pale brows at Rane. He put the phone to his ear. "Looking for your girlfriend, Detective Garretson?" Jon must have responded because Simon's lips thinned in an oily smile that sent chills skittering down her spine. His voice dripped with disdain. "Has the line been open long enough for you to pinpoint this phone's location? Why don't you and your brother come? Get here soon enough and maybe there's a chance you can play hero."

He paused, clearly enjoying his power play. "In a few moments she'll be tied to a propane tank with a short fuse. Maybe you'll get to her in time and she won't be blown into, what do they call it when a person explodes? Oh, yes, pink mist. You wouldn't want Rane to become pink mist."

Rane leaned forward and called out, "Jon, it's a trap. Be careful."

Simon shot out a hand and delivered a blow across her cheek. Jon must have heard it, because Simon, phone to his ear, responded. "Calm yourself. That's the least that will happen to Miss Smith. This is all your fault, you know. You and your brother's. You should have made a deal with me. I wanted Kyle and the rest of my family safe and a deal would have given me that. But now you are going to suffer. The funny thing is you'll race to get here thinking you'll rescue her and I've no intention of allowing that. But you'll try, saps that you are."

He listened for a moment, pale eyes narrowing.

"Watch what you say to me or I'll make the fuse even shorter. You want that chance to see your girlfriend before she dies, Detective Garretson, then you better hurry." He paused a moment, then added, "I like incentives, so here's yours. Be here in fifteen minutes or I'll slice her like your bastard brother sliced me. Make her bleed a little. I always like it when they bleed."

Simon disconnected and handed the phone to Mick. "Remember the plan. Make sure Pete keeps watch and knows to wait until the cops are in the building to hit the detonator." He nodded toward the unconscious Juan. "He can't be trusted. Tie him and make sure he goes up with it."

"You're not blowing her up, then?"

"No. We stick with the original plan. She needs to suffer for what she did to my brother. What I told Garretson was designed to get those idiots here."

At Mick's nod, Simon stepped around the still form on the floor. He stopped, his pale gaze on Rane. "I'm taking her to the boat. We leave as soon as the place blows." He shifted his attention to Mick. "I expect our resourceful police detectives will be here within ten minutes. Pete needs to get in position." Simon's gaze returned to Rane, and she saw something cunning move behind his eyes. "The truth is, I think your phone call was quite fortuitous. I didn't have to do a thing to lure them into the open. You took care of that little challenge for me."

Simon gripped her arm, his fingers a steel clamp biting into the flesh above her elbow and pushed her in front of him.

Pete moved down the hall to join them. "Boss, everything's set up." She could see him eyeing Juan.

"Help drag this piece of garbage over by the propane tanks. He'll have a front row seat for the explosion. Is the hood on the mannequin?"

"Yeah, boss. They won't be able to tell it's not her until they're close and then we'll have them."

"Good."

The man nodded and leaned over Juan, who had begun moving on the floor as he regained consciousness. Mick reached down to pull him to a sitting position and quickly used a zip tie to secure his hands behind his back. As Simon dragged her down the hall, Rane could hear the alarm in Juan's voice as he realized his dangerous predicament.

She hesitated and Simon jerked her arm. "Let's go, Rane. I'm done wasting my time. We're ending it today. I'll deal with you, and I'll deal with the Garretson's, once and for all."

"Why don't you leave me here, have me go up in the warehouse explosion? Why take me on a boat?"

As always, his smile made her skin crawl. "Because, my dear Rane, I want you to know when they're dead. I want you to see the explosion, hear it, and know your hero is dead. As I said, it's important to me that you suffer for what you and your father did to my family. Then it's a simple enough task to throw you overboard when we're out over the water. Maybe I'll throw in a little chum, attract some sharks. Or I could slice you up a bit first. They say great whites have an extremely acute sense of smell and can detect even miniscule amounts of blood. I'm looking forward to watching."

Stomach roiling, Rane forced herself to think of anything that might stall Simon. "Where's Kyle?"

"Where he can't get into trouble. My brother will not help you, He's made the correct choice. His loyalty is to his family. He knows you're expendable, that you have always been expendable. He was weak, but prison has toughened him up."

Simon pushed open a door and Rane blinked in the bright light. More time had passed than she'd realized. The early afternoon sun had burned off the fog and glinted on the sparkling water. Gulls wheeled overhead and the briny smell of the docks permeated the air. A beautiful Seattle day and the deranged monster standing beside her was planning her murder. She had to believe Jon and Nathan would be okay. She'd told them she thought Simon was planning on taking her to a boat. Maybe they wouldn't even go to the warehouse. They were smart, they wouldn't underestimate Simon.

Maybe, just maybe, they'd all get out of this alive.

Still gripping her arm, Simon pushed her ahead of him away from the warehouse and toward the docks. Rane's gaze darted around, looking for a way out. It was only Simon but she didn't know if he was armed. She'd have to assume he was, but if she could take him by surprise, maybe she could find a chance and get away from him. They crossed to the wooden dock where fishing boats bobbed in their moorings. She eyed the murky water. If she had a chance, she would push him off the dock and into the water, then run.

As if reading her mind, Simon pulled her roughly toward him. "Don't even think about trying to get away, Rane," he hissed in her ear. "I have plans for you. Then after you've been eaten by the sharks, I'm going after your old man. He's not getting away with sending my brother to prison for something he didn't do."

"My dad may have planted the heroin that sent Kyle to prison, but your brother committed plenty of crimes he didn't go to prison for." Rane's thoughts raced as she wondered how far she could push him. If she could make Simon lose control, maybe an opportunity for escape would present itself. "Kyle killed people, he killed Savannah."

"Ah, I see you finally got the story. But Kyle didn't kill Savannah Montague, Savannah killed herself."

"He fed her addiction."

"Maybe, but she knew exactly what she was doing. That's why she was injecting between her toes, so nobody would see the track marks. That shows a high level of awareness. She killed herself."

"You're rationalizing. If she hadn't had access to heroin, she wouldn't be dead. Kyle was as responsible as you were. Not only for Savannah, but for all the people who've died because of your brand of poison."

Simon's grip tightened. "You're not doing yourself any favors by trying to anger me." He stopped next to a good-sized fishing boat, the name painted in red block lettering reading *Heaven's Bounty*.

Rane looked at the boat. She didn't want to get on that. Once she was on board she'd be trapped and the only way to escape would be over the side. Simon's eerily pale eyes remained intent on her, shaking her confidence. She tried to focus on their conversation, to think of anything that would delay them boarding the boat.

"Is that how you sleep at night? By convincing yourself you're not responsible for all the heroin overdoses, for all the wrecked lives? They're junkies, they do it to themselves, that's your lame rationalization. You're simply a businessman providing a service."

She saw the anger in his expression, tamped down behind the bland exterior. "Don't provoke me."

She pressed on. "You're delusional. Even Kyle has said so. You're nothing more than another of the vile rats preying on the sick and weak."

Simon moved quickly, pulling her back against him where she could feel a sharp prick at her side. She sucked in a breath as he chuckled nastily. She hadn't known he had a knife. She'd thought he would strike out in anger, maybe give her the opportunity to get away from him, but she'd miscalculated. Fighting growing panic, she jerked away, trying to twist from his grasp. She let out a cry of pain when the blade cut through her clothing to slice into the skin below her ribcage.

"Get on the boat." His voice was a hiss in her ear. "I like doing that. I like making people bleed. That slice was shallow, probably didn't even go all the way through the skin. The next one will go deeper, maybe I'll make it deep enough to slice into muscle. That would make me happy."

At that moment, an explosion rocked marina. Rane looked up to see a fireball fill the sky and then a cloud of dense smoke and debris billowing from the warehouse they'd left. The shockwave hit them and boats swayed back and forth. There must've been several propane tanks to make an explosion that big.

Anxiety clutched at her stomach. Jon and Nathan couldn't have gone into the warehouse. But Simon's orders had been not to detonate unless Mick was sure they were inside. Simon smiled, lips thinning. "On the boat, Rane. Your boyfriend won't be able to help you now."

He pushed her toward a ladder along the side of the boat and, mind still reeling, she gripped it to pull herself up to the deck, numb to the pain from the cut to her side. She stood on the deck and watched dark smoke rising into the air, worry gnawing holes in her empty stomach. Running feet approached the vessel and Rane looked over the side. The disappointment when she saw Mick hit her so keenly she felt faint.

Once Mick climbed aboard, Simon gave the orders. "Get this thing started. I want to be out of the marina before a bunch of idiots gather to watch the fire." He pushed her through a door and down a flight of steps into the bowels of the boat. The whole thing smelled of rotting fish. A rumbling sounded as the engine roared to life and the floor vibrated beneath her feet. Simon flipped a switch at the bottom of the stairs and lights sprang on. Rane looked around warily.

The belly of the vessel was crammed with crates, and she'd bet a month's pay they were full of heroin. This must be how Simon delivered to his dealers up and down the coast. She guessed it was much easier to move undetected by sea than by land. Since he wasn't even trying to hide the contraband, she figured he wasn't too worried about being stopped and searched.

Rane's stomach sank as the engine revved higher and she could feel the motion of the boat backing from its berth.

"Over here." Simon pushed her toward an opening at the far end of the hold. "Get in there."

Rane hesitated, "Please, let me—"

"No more bargaining, bitch." He shoved her forward and Rane went through the darkened door and landed on her knees. She turned around in time to have the door slammed in her face, shutting out the light. Something heavy was pushed across the door, effectively blocking any escape. She could feel the vibration as the boat picked up speed as it headed out into Elliot Bay.

Chapter Sixteen

Rane's stomach rolled, and she fought the nausea rising in her throat. The unrelieved darkness pressed down over her in the cold, damp compartment. Gaining her feet, she felt along the wall, hoping to find a light switch. After several minutes of fumbling, she realized the switch was probably on the wall outside the door. She found the door handle, turned it, and gave a mighty push. The door didn't budge. Whatever Simon had slid across it to block her escape stood solid.

Rane continued heaving against the door until, finally exhausted, she leaned back against it. Slowly she lowered her body to sit on the floor, resting her forehead against her upraised knees, and using the cuff of her jacket to angrily wipe away her tears.

She wasn't a quitter, she'd keep fighting. In a minute. She always figured she could find a way out of any situation. Even when Simon had terrified her half to death, she always held the thought in the back of her mind that she would figure it out. She could think her way out of whatever danger presented itself. Until now. She wasn't sure she could get herself out of this situation.

The image of the fiery explosion at the warehouse played like a loop behind her lids. She wouldn't believe Jon and Nathan were gone. They were too smart, and Simon was too cocksure.

She wished she and Jon hadn't argued the last time they'd spoken. She wished he was here with her now. She never felt as safe as when she was with him. Miserable, she wiped her cheeks with her damp sleeve. Her side throbbed where Simon had cut her. She couldn't examine it, but it felt superficial. Still, blood soaked her shirt and it hurt. Add to that, hunger had her feeling lightheaded. She tried to remember the last time she'd eaten. Tilly's Diner with Jon. They'd sat and talked like any couple, and then there'd been the motorcycle ride back to Seattle, holding onto him as they'd ridden through the night. It seemed so long ago.

She rubbed her forehead. The headache brewing behind her eyes was likely caused by missing her morning jolt of caffeine. And, of course, she had to pee. She really couldn't see anyone letting her use a bathroom this time.

The boat must have reached open water because the pitching and rocking motion increased, making Rane glad her increasingly queasy stomach was empty. She lifted her head. She couldn't sit here waiting for her fate. She couldn't give up.

Standing, she braced her shoulder against the door, set her feet, and once more gave a mighty shove. At the same moment the boat rocked heavily and the barrier in front of the door shifted. Encouraged, she pushed again, straining with all her might.

Panting, she vowed if she ever got out of this mess she'd spend more time at the gym working on core-strengthening exercises. Taking a deep breath, she set her body and again gave a giant shove. The barrier yielded a bit more, the door opening a fraction wider. All she needed was another six inches and she bet she could get through. What she'd do when she got out she hadn't a clue but at least she'd have options.

Fighting exhaustion, she finally managed to force the door open wide enough that she could squeeze through the opening. The light was still on and she stood motionless, ears pricked for any sound. Her gaze darted around the hold.

She needed a weapon, anything that might give her a fighting chance. Carefully she made her way around the compartment, keeping an ear out for anyone coming down the steps. The wooden crates were piled three high but weren't tied down. The lid of one was loose and she lifted it to peer inside. Brownish bundles of what she thought was black tar heroin were tightly wrapped in plastic. Hard to believe this innocuous-looking substance formed the basis for so much pain and misery.

Disgusted, she continued her search for a weapon. Her experience on boats was fairly limited, but she'd gone ocean fishing with her father a few times. She remembered when she was a child and he'd patiently taken her through his friend's boat, identifying the equipment, explaining nautical terms. Then there'd been the rush of excitement when he'd helped her reel in a halibut.

Putting the memory aside, she spotted a long wooden storage box bolted to the floor along the far wall. She went to her knees in front of the box to raise the lid and felt her spirits kick up when she saw it held a variety of tools. Pulling out a crowbar and a hammer, she figured they wouldn't stop a bullet but might give her an advantage in a hand to hand fight.

The boat pitched again and she froze. A noise, barely audible against the backdrop of the engine, sounded from behind her. Rising slowly to her feet, she quickly slid the crowbar through a belt loop in her jeans to hang at her side. Gripping the hammer so tightly her fingers ached, she scanned the hold, looking for the source of the noise.

"Rane."

Her heart dipped. "Kyle?"

He stepped from behind a stack of crates. She clutched the hammer tighter. "What are you doing here? Does Simon know you're on board?"

"No. No one knows I'm here."

Would he help her? Would he fight against his brother and help her to survive? She rushed to say, "Simon means to kill me. He blew up the warehouse and I think he's planning on throwing me overboard. I'm not sure you'd be safe if he finds you here."

"I know he wants to kill you. That's why I came."

Rane could feel a trembling start deep in her belly. "I don't want to die, Kyle. I really don't want to die."

"Will you go away with me if I can get you out of this? I love you, Rane. We could go somewhere away from Simon, away from this horrible business, and start a new life together." She relaxed her grip on the hammer. She could see the toll the last few years had taken on him. He looked gaunt in the dim light, skin drawn tight across his pale face, forehead gleaming with sweat. Then it hit her with sudden certainty, and she knew he was using. He had the hollow-eyed look of an addict. The irony wasn't lost on her. Simon's business was killing his brother.

Unless Kyle broke free from the noose that was his heroin addiction, he wouldn't survive. "You're sick, Kyle. Let's get out of this mess and get you into treatment."

"Is that it? I tell you I love you and your answer is that I need treatment? I don't want treatment. I want for us to start a new life together." She could see him trembling and recognized the symptoms of withdrawals.

A faint thud sounded against the side of the vessel, but she had no idea what that could mean. The engine kept up a steady pace. She hoped that meant they hadn't reached where Simon intended to kill her.

"We need to go up, try to overpower them. We're trapped if we stay down here."

"No." Kyle looked panicked. "Simon will kill us for sure. There's enough room behind these crates for both of us. We hide and hit them from behind when they come to get you."

"We can't stay down here. It's too cramped. There's no room to maneuver even if we did manage to take their guns away. We have to go up and try to catch them by surprise. I think it's only Simon and Mick on board. We might have a chance."

Rane turned to rummage in the toolbox. She pulled out a pole with a wicked looking hook on the end, an implement she remembered her dad identifying as a fishing gaff. "Here, take this." She hoped her judgment was accurate, and that Kyle was really on her side.

Kyle took the weapon, and Rane realized how difficult confronting Simon would be for him. Perhaps too difficult. If he used the weapon as she thought might be necessary, then he would need to seriously injure, if not kill, his brother. Worrying her bottom lip, she studied him warily. He held the gaff like it was a bomb set to detonate at any moment.

"Kyle." He jerked, the gleam of sweat along his temple. She gentled her voice. "Stay down here while I peek my head up top and see if I can figure out what's going on. I need to see where Simon and Mick are. I'll be back."

When he didn't respond she took his arm and led him back to where he'd been hidden behind the crates. "Wait here." It was clear she wouldn't be able to count on him. She had a moment's debate as to whether she would be better off with the gaff but decided it was too unwieldy, so she left it with Kyle and started up the stairs.

A heavy door blocked off the top of the steps, probably to keep out sea water. She pushed gently, wanting only to open it far enough to see if anyone was nearby. She braced herself against the rocking of the boat and put her eye to the slim opening. She expected bright sunlight, and it took a moment to realize the hazy light was due to the sun hanging low in the sky. Seeing no one she pushed the door a little wider. What she could see of the back of the boat was clear. Mick and Simon were probably on the bridge. The engine continued its steady droning which meant they were still moving and the boat would need to be steered. She allowed the door to shut and clambered down the steps.

"Kyle, I'm going up on the deck."

She rounded the crates to find him huddled with his arms around his knees, body shaking. He lifted his head, his eyes haunted. "Be careful."

A moment later, Rane slipped through the door, closing it softly behind her. Taking a glance around, she spied the large winch with its coils of fishnet at the stern. Taking a quick breath, she darted across the open space and crouched behind the nets. She peered around them to scan the front of the boat. A light shone from the bridge and she could see two figures facing the bow. Perhaps the boat had a dinghy, or even life vests. She couldn't see her crazy idea of overpowering Simon and Mick working, especially because Kyle's help was far from certain. She was pretty sure he'd be on her side, but he was in bad shape and the longer he went without a hit, the shakier he'd get.

She looked across the bay. The Seattle skyline in the distance reflected the lowering sun. Over her shoulder, closer, she could make out the silhouette of Bainbridge Island. She was a strong swimmer; if she had something to hold onto she could do it. Maybe she could find a floatation device and slip into the water undetected, then swim toward Bainbridge. Hypothermia would be an issue, but maybe she'd get lucky and a passing boat would pick her up. Once she was able, she would call to get help for Kyle.

A cold breeze blew in from the ocean and Rane suppressed a shiver. Her plan was plain crazy. She knew it, but waiting for Simon to kill her wasn't going to happen.

Watching the men on the bridge, Rane ran to the walkway on the starboard side. A red and white life preserver hung on the inside of the rail. That might work if there was nothing else, but a life vest and an inflatable raft were infinitely preferable. She paused when she heard a sound, like something rubbing, from the side of the boat. Unsure what was making the noise, she surreptitiously glanced over the railing. An inflatable boat was tethered to the side. It had a small outboard motor as well as oars laying across the bottom. It seemed

Simon and Mick planned on using it. They were going to be disappointed. Eyeing the distance, she judged she could drop into the water, swim to the dinghy, untie it, and she'd be on her way before anyone knew she had it.

She set the crowbar and hammer on the deck, hooked one leg over the rail and shifted to swing the other over…and stifled a scream when suddenly she was grabbed from behind. An arm with an iron grip grasped her around the waist, a rough hand clamping over her mouth. She was pulled off the rail and dragged backward through the open door of a cabin.

Rane bucked and twisted and at the same time tried to open her jaw so she could clamp down on the fingers over her mouth. They'd found her, but she wasn't going down without a fight. Using her nails, she dug into the hand over her mouth while at the same time kicking back, her heel connecting with her captor's knee.

A grunt was followed by a hoarse whisper. "Rane."

A feeling of relief so acute she thought she'd pass out coursed through her. The hands gripping her turned her around and the next thing she knew her mouth was taken in a wild, frantic kiss. "Jon." She breathed his name when he finally released her lips.

Clutching his shoulders tightly, she thought she would crawl into him if she could. He fused hard lips once again to hers, desperation evident as he molded her body to his. Her hands reached under his clothing to rub the warm skin along his ribs. She needed to feel him, to get the reassurance he was truly there. She paused when she brushed against his gun in its shoulder holster and reality resurfaced. She pulled back to look at him. In the dim light she could see the glint of his eyes.

"You're alive." Her words were uttered on a shaky breath.

Long fingers threaded through her hair and calloused thumbs stroked her jaw. He tipped her head back once more and spoke against her lips. "I'm never letting you out of my sight again. Ever." He kissed her and Rane thought there had never been a kiss more steeped in fear and passion.

"Do you think you kids could hold that until later? We're not exactly out of the woods yet."

Jon settled his hands on her shoulders and she felt him take a steadying breath. "Yeah, okay." He turned to his brother. "What did you see?"

Nathan came into the shadowed room. "Simon and another guy on the bridge. We're heading out toward the Sound so I'm guessing that's where they're planning to dump this one overboard." He frowned as he eyed Rane. "Glad to see you, darlin', but do you want to tell us what all that blood is from?"

She glanced down at the direction of his gaze. Her shirt and jacket were already caked with dried blood, but now she could see the deep red soaking into the top of her jeans.

"Holy Christ, Rane." Jon tugged up the hem of her shirt to reveal the shallow gash below her ribs, now oozing sluggishly. He whirled on Nathan. "Forget those two. Let's get her into the dinghy and to a hospital."

"No, it's shallow. The bleeding started up again when you grabbed me. It'll stop in a minute. Kyle's in the hold and needs help. He's not a threat. Also, there's enough heroin down there to put Simon away for the rest of his life."

A shout from the deck made the decision for them. The dinghy had been discovered. Running feet approached along the walkway and with movement as stealthy as a trained assassin, Nathan crouched in the darkened opening to the cabin and when the man came into view he struck. He went in low and took him down in a rolling tumble.

Jon pushed Rane back so he could help his brother, but she could see he didn't need help. With surprise on his side, Nathan had knocked the guy out cold before he likely knew what hit him. Together the two men pulled the limp form into the cabin.

"It's Mick. He's related to Simon and Kyle. He's one of the men who grabbed me this morning."

Jon grunted as he pulled handcuffs from the back of his belt. With Nathan keeping an eye out, they pushed Mick to the back of the cabin. "Hope he doesn't come around too quick. I don't have anything to gag him with and he could make a lot of noise."

It wouldn't matter because Rane could hear Simon calling Mick's name. "He'll come looking for him in a second." Silence descended when the engines were cut off and the boat lost its forward momentum.

"Yeah." Jon nodded at Nathan. Obviously knowing each other's moves, they both pulled their guns free of their holsters and from the cover of the doorway, checked to be sure they were clear. Jon spared her a glance. "Stay here, sweetheart." Not waiting for her agreement, they slipped through the door and out of sight.

Simon must've realized something was up because he didn't call out again. He wouldn't want to pinpoint his location. Long minutes passed and Rane was jumping out of her skin with worry. She peeked through the doorway and spied the hammer and crowbar where she'd left them. She crouched down and slipped across the deck to pick them up. At least she wouldn't feel so defenseless.

She glanced left and right along the walkway and saw no one. The sun had set and lights from the bridge and along the rails cast a faint glow in the darkening twilight.

In the distance she could see lights shining from another boat that seemed to be coming closer. She eased back with the thought to return to the cabin and stay out of the way when, for the second time in less than an hour, she was grabbed roughly from behind.

***

Jon stood motionless at the base of the stairs, senses alert to anything that would give away Simon's location. Nathan crept silently up the treads and peeked into the bridge, then turned and with a shake of his head motioned to Jon it was empty. With hand gestures, Jon indicated he would search starboard and Nathan would search aft. A ghost of sound reached him and he immediately swung his gun toward the source of the noise.

His heart stumbled in his chest.

Simon stood near the door to the hold, clutching Rane from behind, a wicked looking knife biting into her neck over the carotid artery. A thin trickle of dark blood stained her pale skin where the knife had nicked her. The entreaty in her eyes tore at him. He fought to control his breathing, to focus his thinking. Fear nearly overwhelmed him and he struggled to force it back. He'd trained for this, so had Nathan. Jon would need to call on all his training to get her free and keep her alive.

He spoke, keeping emotion out of his voice. "Put down the knife and let Rane go. You're done. The Coast Guard is almost here. There's no way out of this for you."

"She's my way out of this. Call that brother of yours and you two give me your guns. If you don't do what I tell you her blood will spray all over this deck."

Jon sucked in a breath when Simon wrenched back Rane's head, further exposing her neck. Keeping his eyes on Jon, Simon pulled back Rane's hair so he could nuzzle her neck. "She's beautiful, isn't she, Detective Garretson? She smells so sweet, like sunshine. You've had some of this, haven't you? I guess that's what's called going above and beyond the call of duty. I bet all the guys wanted in on the sweet gig you had." Jon didn't let his concentration falter as Simon continued his taunting. "I don't really want to kill her, you know. But sometimes there are unpleasant costs in this business."

Gaze focused, Jon didn't let it waver by so much as a flicker when Nathan moved into place about ten feet behind Simon. With his peripheral vision Jon could see movement in the shadowed doorway of the hold. Shit. It had to be Kyle, and that made things a whole lot more complicated.

Jon slowly edged across the deck, forcing Simon to shift to keep him in sight, but also making it less likely he'd see Nathan or Kyle.

"Stay where you are, Garretson," Simon screamed. He was losing control. "I told you to call your brother, I want you both where I can see you."

Jon halted his movement and bit back an oath when he saw Rane's hand slide to the crowbar hanging from her belt. Simon must have felt the move because he tightened his grip, all but crooning in her ear. "Rane, you don't want to do anything that would end things for you, do you? Do you want your boyfriend to see you spurting blood from an artery? To see you die?"

"You think they'll let you live if you kill me? They'll take you apart." Rane's voice came out strong and clear and Jon silently applauded her. She wasn't letting the bastard win.

Simon seemed to grow tired of waiting because he pressed the knife deeper into her skin and blood flowed freely. "Put down your gun, asshole. Kick it over to me."

Jon shifted to set down his gun, but as he crouched he caught a quick movement from the doorway. In a split-second the scene turned chaotic. Simon's hand holding the knife against Rane's throat suddenly jerked back and in the dim light Jon saw Kyle gripping a fishing gaff he'd somehow managed to hook around his brother's arm.

Rane wrenched away, and Simon struck back blindly with the hand still clutching the knife. The moment Rane was free Jon lunged headfirst and swept her in a forward roll, taking them behind the giant coil of fishing net. He glanced back and saw the glint of the knife as it slashed across the dark form that had emerged from the hold.

He pushed Rane down on the deck and growled, "Stay put, and this time do what I say." He glanced back around the netting in time to see Simon reeling back, arms wide, knife still in his grip. A still form lay on the deck, a dark pool spreading from beneath it.

"You made me kill him," Simon shrieked. "You made me kill my brother." He must have caught sight of Nathan and he lunged. Rapid blasts of gunfire exploded into the night and Jon felt the recoil of the gun in his hand.

Simon staggered against the rail, and with his arms wheeling, he tipped backwards into the water, and was gone.

Chapter Seventeen

Rane wrapped the blanket tightly around her shoulders. The deck was a blur of activity that hadn't subsided from the moment two Coast Guard ships had flanked *Heaven's Bounty*. Kyle's body had been zipped into a black bag while Simon's had been fished out of the ocean and brought aboard one of the ships. She'd seen them pull the body out of the sea and knew the evil bastard was dead, probably had been before he'd hit the water, but it somehow seemed surreal. Mick had regained consciousness and was moved onto a Coast Guard ship in cuffs. The threat from Simon DiNardo had been so huge and in a split second it had vanished. It might take some time for the reality to sink in that the dark cloud that had hung over her head for years was no longer a threat.

Coast Guard officers had boarded Simon's boat and were currently talking with Jon and Nathan while seamen busily moved in and out of the hold, cataloguing the illegal haul of heroin. Given the tone of the discussion, she figured the man who had introduced himself as Commander Rocklin wasn't happy, and from Nathan's body language she could tell *he* wasn't happy being dressed down.

She approached the group as Jon put a restraining hand on his brother's shoulder. He spoke in a firm voice, smoothing over Nathan's aggressive response. "Yes, sir. We understand we should have waited for the Coast Guard, that this is your jurisdiction."

"Damn right it is, and you two hot shots were explicitly told not to take off in that dinghy until the Coast Guard was in place to support the operation. You defied a direct order and your supervisor will hear about it."

Nathan looked ready to snarl out a response Rane thought probably included "fuck you." Jon tightened his grip on his brother and said, "We understand, sir."

Nathan shook off the restraining hand and stalked to the stern of the ship. She left Jon placating the commander and followed Nathan.

He stood with his hands on his hips, jacket open, seemingly oblivious to the cold wind blowing off the water.

"Thank you." She shivered under the blanket, not really sure if it was from cold or reaction to the violence she'd lived and witnessed.

He gave her a long look. "Sorry about Kyle. I don't know how we could have prevented that, but I'm sorry we didn't."

Rane sighed. "I'm sorry, too. He was messed up. He'd finally decided to break with Simon. He wanted the chance to start over. I think he was addicted to heroin, so that would have tripped him up down the road." Something was puzzling her so she asked the question. "How did you know where to find me? That I was on this boat?"

"Your dad. We went to see him, find out if he could tell us anything about the DiNardos. Jon talked to him, asked him if there was any place they would hide out, and he said "Heaven's Bounty." Didn't know what the hell he was talking about until Jon figured it must mean a boat. After that it was easy."

She shook her head in amazement. "Dad pulled through when you needed him to. I'm glad you guys thought to ask him."

Nathan nodded and his gaze shifted back to his brother. He cocked his head toward him. "Don't hurt him. He's gone for you, and I don't want to see him hurt."

"I love him." She drew in a shaky breath. "Wow. I didn't even think that was in my head until it popped out."

Nathan's grin flashed, making him look suddenly boyish. "Good. That's real good. He deserves to have someone love him. I'm glad it's you."

She suddenly felt uncertain. "I hope he thinks it's a good thing, too. Please don't say anything to him. I'm not sure what our relationship will be without the police stuff that brought us together. I need some time to think it through."

Nathan stepped toward her and wrapped her in a hug. "He's the best man I know," he said, his voice muffled against her hair. "He's crazy about you. You'll be fine." He kissed the top of her head and let her go. "Thanks for helping me calm down."

She wished she had Nathan's confidence.

The realization she was in love with Jon had been growing steadily for days but she'd ignored the feelings. With all the violence and threats they'd faced it was possible, even likely, that for both of them emotions had been manipulated by circumstances.

What had Simon said? That guys like Jon need to be the hero, to have women rely on them? Simon was hardly the best judge of character, but she wondered if he was right about that. Jon had put himself between her and danger countless times and she wondered if once things settled down, once his emotions weren't always heightened by the instinct to protect her, he'd start to pull back.

She shivered and looked out over the water where a thick layer of fog had moved in like a dark blanket that felt oppressive and smothering.

***

Soon after she'd spoken with Nathan the commander decided to separate her, Nathan, and Jon. Rane guessed that was probably standard procedure in an officer-involved shooting. They'd all been assigned a minder and been sequestered in separate cabins on one of the Coast Guard ships. A medic had applied temporary bandages to her injuries, she'd had a chance to pee, and been given a cup of hot soup she'd consumed ravenously. Feeling warmer and steadier, all she wanted was to see Jon. She knew *he* was fine, but she needed to know *they* were fine. Since he'd be busy dealing with the ramifications of the shooting for some time, she'd have to be patient.

Waiting gave her time to think, and it was there in the stark ship's cabin that she came to a decision. She was glad she and Jon hadn't said anything, hadn't made any commitments to each other that could make the situation more difficult. After she did what she must do, he might not be able to forgive her. She hoped she'd have a chance to tell him before talking to Denton, but with that unlikely, she'd face whatever ramifications ensued on her own.

The next hours proved exhausting. *Heaven's Bounty* was towed through the darkness into port by a Coast Guard vessel and to her surprise, news crews had gathered, camera flashes going off the minute the crew began disembarking. Floodlights illuminated the scene and Rane followed slowly behind the gurneys laden with heavy black bags. The Coast Guard seaman assigned to her escorted her off the ship and thankfully away from the crowd of reporters.

A police car sat idling at the end of the dock and soon she was riding silently to the hospital. Her injuries hadn't required stitches but Commander Rocklin had wanted her to be checked out, so to St. Augustine's she went.

She snagged Lily as her nurse and while her friend examined her injuries, she filled her in on the events of the day. Finally, she was able to put on the Coast Guard t-shirt and sweatshirt a seaman had given her to replace her blood-soaked clothing. The tight hug goodbye she gave Lily had her friend raising her eyebrows in question.

"You okay, honey?"

"Yeah." She wasn't, but she hurried away and returned to the cruiser for a ride to the police station.

Rane thought she'd never been more wrung out than after she'd gone over the events of the day at least four times. An officer questioned her, and she answered. Back and forth. When she explained in detail how she'd planted the heroin in Kyle's car that had sent him to prison, a detective came in to question her. There had simply been no other option. She couldn't allow her father to be put on trial, no matter how remote the possibility given his diagnosis.

Denton joined the detective and asked his own questions, questions that suggested he knew her father's involvement, but she thought she answered them plausibly. What seemed like hours later she stood in the hallway outside the interrogation rooms, trying to pay attention to Denton explaining what she could expect over the next couple days. "You're dead on your feet so you need to go on home. Can you be back here by ten hundred tomorrow? I should be able to let you know the DA's decision by then."

At her jerky nod he put a hand on her elbow. "I'll walk you out front, your ride is out there."

She thought they'd called a cab or assigned an officer to take her home but when she got to the front steps she saw Jon sitting in his black truck. He got out and opened the passenger door, his movements abrupt.

"She's beat." Denton sounded tired, too. It had been a long day for all of them. "Glad you got your girl back."

"Yeah."

Rane frowned at the terse response.

Denton left them and she climbed into the truck. Jon pulled into traffic, driving silently through the streets. When he didn't say a word, worry began to gnaw at her stomach with hungry teeth. He pulled into her driveway and turned off the engine, sitting motionless for a long moment in the sudden quiet. Rane could hear Cooper barking from the backyard.

"Rane, you—"

"I need to go check on Cooper. He'll be hungry."

She didn't know why she suddenly felt so self-conscious. He hadn't given her any reason to question his feelings for her. Well, other than that he had never told her his feelings. When he found her, in the heat of the moment he'd been worried, frantic even, but that could be, well, the heat of the moment. Now he seemed so remote, and angry. She opened the truck door to a light drizzle and crossed to the kitchen door, stopping when she realized she didn't have her keys. In fact, she didn't have a lot of things. Her purse, cell, clothes, had all been left at the safe house. Was that only this morning?

Jon approached and reached around her to unlock the door. Once inside he stopped her with a hand on her arm. His tone was flat when he said, "Go on up. Take a shower, put on something loose over those bandages. I'll take care of the dog."

She nodded mutely and went upstairs. When she came down thirty minutes later, she had to admit she felt better. The acetaminophen they'd given her at the hospital had reduced the pain from her injuries to a dull ache and the shower had washed away some of her exhaustion.

She'd shampooed her hair in the shower and applied new bandages to her neck and side, pulled on sweatpants, a thermal, and warm socks, and felt human again. She stepped into the kitchen to find Jon at the counter buttering toast. Two plates sat on the table piled with scrambled eggs and slices of Canadian bacon. A mug of tea sat steaming next to her usual chair. She blinked back sudden tears.

She was really a mess if Jon making her a simple dinner choked her up. Cooper launched himself at her and she dropped to her knees to meet his enthusiastic greeting, stifling a groan when he rubbed his head against her bandaged side.

The butter knife hit the counter with a metallic clatter as Jon spun around. "That's it. That's fuckin' it." He hauled Cooper back by his collar, pointed a long finger and said, "Stay," before whirling on her.

"What the hell are you thinking, letting him jump on you like that?"

Rane looked at him in confusion. "What are you talking about? Cooper doesn't understand I'm hurt. It's not that bad, anyway."

Jon reached down and pulled her to her feet, his hands gentle despite his angry tone. "That's my point exactly. You need to take better care of yourself. Not put yourself in a position where you could get hurt. You shouldn't crouch down where he can knock into you."

"Jon, I'm fine."

"The hell you are. You are *not* fine. I saw what that bastard did to you. He cut you. You bled."

"Yeah, I bled, but I'm fine now. There will hardly be a scar the cuts are so shallow." She narrowed her eyes at him. "You think it's my fault Simon got to me. Do you think I put myself in a position where I was hurt?"

He stabbed his fingers through his hair, looking like he could easily pull out a fistful. "No. I know you didn't. That was all Ty. He was working for the DiNardos. But it about killed me when Simon had that knife to your throat."

He turned back to the counter and Rane took a step toward him. "Jon, I—"

"Sit down. Your dinner is getting cold." He said the words with the careful control of someone on the edge.

Deciding she didn't want to deal with his mood and with her own confused feelings, she did what he'd asked and sat at the table. She needed to tell him what she'd told Denton, but if getting bumped by Cooper set him off, she thought she could wait to tell him about her confession. He knew the heroin had been planted in Kyle's car, but didn't have proof that it had been her dad.

She ate her eggs and toast, exhaustion returning to drag at her. By the time she finished the meal and was sipping her tea she could hardly keep her eyes open.

His voice quiet, Jon said, "Go on up to bed. I'll clean up here."

"You've got to be worn out too. We can leave this for the morning."

"I said I'll take care of it."

Lacking the energy to argue she trudged up the stairs, took a moment to brush her teeth, and climbed into bed. She fell asleep wondering if Jon would join her.

***

Rane yawned and stretched, wincing as the bandages pulled, reminding her of everything that had happened the day before. A long, horrible day. As consciousness set in, she felt a warm shoulder beneath her cheek, and a heavy arm encircling her back. She glanced up to find bright blue eyes focused intently on her.

"Jon."

She lifted her head and he brought up a hand to brush the hair from her forehead. "I'm sorry."

"Mmm, that's nice," she hummed. "For what?"

"For acting like an idiot last night. I've always felt like I can handle anything, but I couldn't handle you."

She frowned. "I really don't think you need to handle me. I can handle myself."

He growled under his breath. "That's not what I meant. I couldn't handle you in danger. You with a knife to your neck, bleeding. I needed to keep control and I was having trouble with that. In the end I had to compartmentalize it. Lock my fear for you away in a corner of my brain so I could figure out how to get you free. In the end it was Kyle who saved your life."

She propped herself up on her elbows. "Is that why you were upset, because Kyle saved me?"

"No. For the rest of my life, I'll thank God he did. It's that I keep seeing you in the hands of a crazy man who could've killed you."

"He didn't." She hesitated. "You may've felt you weren't in control when Simon had me, but you were. You did what you had to do. You kept your head."

Jon's eyes drifted closed for a long moment before opening them again to look at her. "All I could think about was that he could kill you in a split second and I wouldn't be able to stop him."

"He could have, but do you want to know what I remember most clearly? I remember looking at you. Your eyes were so cool, so focused. I wasn't afraid when I saw you like that. It's weird. I was still in danger, this maniac was holding a knife to my throat, but you were there so I wasn't scared."

"Then I was afraid enough for both of us."

"You didn't act afraid. You started moving across the deck and I wondered what you were doing. Then I realized Simon had to turn to keep you in sight and moving like that kept him from realizing Nathan and Kyle were there. Doing that was critical for me to come out of the whole thing alive. Even when I was locked in that dark room on the boat I kept telling myself you and Nathan were too smart to get caught in that explosion, that you would find me."

She paused. "What happened with that, anyway? The guy Pete was told to wait until he was sure you were both in the building before pressing the detonator. I nearly fainted when the warehouse blew up."

He shrugged. "We knew Simon's penchant for explosives. No way were we going in there. Nathan scanned for the best vantage point to watch the warehouse entrance and spotted Simon's guy. I was able to get behind him, but he must have heard me because he jumped and dropped the damned detonator. Caused the whole place to blow. The shockwave knocked me on my ass."

She nodded, then finally decided she couldn't put off telling him any longer. She sat up and pulled the blanket around her shoulders, resting her forehead on her hands for a moment trying to gather courage. It wasn't working.

"Rane?"

She raised her head. "I have to tell you something."

"What?"

"I told Denton last night. I think I convinced him. The DA will have to decide what to do, but I might end up in prison."

"Not likely."

"I know you think my dad planted the heroin in Kyle's car, but it was me." He narrowed his gaze. She took a deep breath and the words came out in a rush. "I planted the heroin in Kyle's car that sent him to prison. I signed a confession last night."

She watched as he pushed himself up against the headboard. He leaned his head back and pinched the bridge of his nose.

"Sweetheart, why the hell did you do that? The DA would never have charged your father. You should have trusted me to deal with this."

"I'm telling you my father was never involved. He had nothing to do with it."

He looked at her with resignation. "Your dad got heroin from another precinct's evidence room and planted it in Kyle's car. The only thing you're guilty of is doing nothing when you found out about it. Denton already knew all that, but now you've gone and made a confession so he'll have to go to the DA."

"You don't know that for sure."

He sighed. "You're trying to protect your dad. I get that, but it's not necessary."

"You don't understand. He would never survive if he was sent to prison. I can't stand the thought of him being alone and scared, not understanding why he's there." Tears stung her eyes.

Jon leaned forward, reaching out to brush moisture from her cheek. "It'll be okay. You'll have to explain why you lied, but after what you went through yesterday, and because Kyle is dead and it can't make any difference to him, I think the DA will be inclined to let sleeping dogs lie. Me, Nathan, Denton, we'll all vouch for you. The DA will be more interested in going after Ty and the rest of the DiNardo organization now that the head of the snake has been cut off."

Rane reached for a pillow to bury her face in. Everything she'd tried to hold in came rushing out in a wave of anguish.

Jon reached over, tugged the pillow away and pulled her into his arms, holding her securely as she struggled to control the tears. "Sweetheart, everything will be all right. I promise."

With her face buried against his chest she spoke with her voice muffled. "You don't know how worried I've been. Ever since I realized what Dad had done I've been scared to death he would be found out. I was frightened about what Kyle would do when he got out of prison, but it was worse. Simon came after me, and scared me to death. Now, finally, it looks like it's done." She lifted her head to see his eyes. "It's been my dad and me for so long, I never looked to anyone else to help us."

His eyes sharpened, focusing intently on hers. "I love you, Rane. I'll always have your back."

She sat up, and felt a little dizzy as his words sank in. "Do you mean it? You have to be sure. You have to be really, really sure."

"I mean it and I'm really, really sure. I'm here. Forever." He traced a finger down her cheek, wiping away the tears. She wanted to tell him she felt the same way too, but fear seized her with dark-tipped claws. "What is it, sweetheart?"

She hesitated, then said, "Love is a tricky thing. My parents were once in love. My mother loved me. What happened to make her un-love me? Do people wake up one day and realize it isn't real anymore? Will that happen to us?"

"I don't know what happened with your parents, and your mother abandoning you is unfathomable. I can't comprehend it. But that's not us. I love you and that's not changing."

Rane saw the truth in his eyes. Life was a risk and she'd been hurt before, but if she let fear turn her away from what could be with this wonderful man who made her breakfast, loved her dog, and kept her safe, then she was turning away from all the possibilities a future with him would hold.

When she thought she could keep her voice steady, she whispered, "I love you, Jon."

He pulled her to him in a crushing grip, his arms wrapped tight around her shoulders. His voice that came out unsteady. "I don't think I could've held out much longer without hearing you say it."

They lay in each other's arms, and she listened to the steady beat of his heart. He moved a hand under her sleep shirt, tracing his fingers up and down her spine. The calming effect of his soothing fingers allowed her mind to settle, and she marveled at the reality that she'd ended up at the place she most wanted to be.

She was sorry for Kyle, and for Juan, and wished both of them could have survived, but she was alive and she intended to live her life to the fullest.

Rane knew it would take her a long time to fully process the horror she'd lived through, but she had the best medicine right here in front of her. She murmured in pleasure when Jon's hand began to move with more purpose, stroking under the elastic of her pajama pants and across her hip with firm pressure. Lifting her head she brushed a kiss across his lips.

Blue eyes burned with quiet intensity and he dipped his head to press his mouth to her jaw.

With movements controlled and careful to avoid the bandages, he made love to her with such focused concentration it made her heart tremble.

Chapter Eighteen

Jon dropped Rane off at the police station at ten. He'd been on the phone to Denton and was told not to come in. It was obvious they wanted to talk with her without his interference.

"I'll be fine." She kissed him. "Really."

"I don't like it." Clearly not happy, he'd finally agreed, telling her he had some things to take care of, including getting her belongings from the safe house.

Rane walked through the double doors of the police station and the calm Jon had worked hard to ensure she found left when she crash landed into the reality that she was a prime suspect in framing a man who'd been convicted of a crime he didn't commit.

She met with several officers, including Denton, a team she figured had been assigned to tie up loose ends. The events of the day before were questioned, examined, and documented. They wouldn't give her much information, but they'd confirmed Ty had been on DiNardo's payroll, and they had him dead to rights. Being knocked on the head when she'd been kidnapped was nothing more than deflection. As calm as Denton always was, even he couldn't keep the pissed-off out of his voice knowing one of his team had turned traitor.

They grilled her about the evidence planted in Kyle's car. This time she told the truth, recanting her confession from the night before. After a couple of hours of that interrogation, the DA arrived. He hadn't been happy with her, and her father, but in the end he agreed that no charges would be filed against her or her dad. By the time she was allowed to leave, she understood what people meant by being put through the ringer.

Nathan gave her a ride home, telling her Jon would touch base with her later. He had her purse and clothes from the safe house. Once home, she took a nap and when she woke, she sighed in frustration when she found she'd missed a call from Jon. When she tried to call him back it went straight to voicemail. The phone rang an hour later and she grabbed it only to find Nathan at the other end. "Oh, it's you."

"You're disappointed. That's cold."

"What are you talking about? You're so fun to talk to."

He gave a bark of laughter. "I know when a woman's placating me. Actually, I have orders to pick you up for dinner tonight."

"Dinner tonight? I thought Jon and I would stay in. You could join us."

"Nope. Little brother says he's sorry he can't pick you up himself but asked me to do the honors. We're meeting the task force and a couple of others from the department, kind of a celebration that the DiNardos won't be polluting our streets with their brand of death any longer."

"I can get behind that."

"Great. Jon's organizing the thing so he says it'll be a little upscale if you want to dress up."

Rane was surprised, figuring the cops she knew would be more comfortable celebrating at a bar or a pizza joint, but she was ready by the appointed time, glad she had something to wear that didn't require a lot of fussing. She'd decided on a short dress of deep green topped by a black jacket. The weather was clear so she decided she could risk the black Jimmy Choo's she'd found at a super sale price.

Nathan pulled up in his sports car and Rane got in. "You're wearing your uniform? Where are we going? What's going on?"

"Uh-uh. I'm not supposed to say."

"Nathan." She shot him her best glare.

He cast her a look from the corner of his eye. "You sure you're not a mom? That's exactly the tone and look my mom used when I was in trouble."

"I bet you heard it a lot. Why the uniform? Why the secrecy? If this is a dinner with cops from the department, it shouldn't matter if I know where we're going."

"You'd think."

Rane grumbled in frustration.

"Sit back and relax, darlin'."

Since it didn't look like she would get any more information from him she complied. When he turned onto the street of her father's facility she frowned. The street was lined with police cars. "What are we doing here? Is something wrong with Dad?"

"Nothing's wrong with your dad. Don't worry."

"But what—"

"You sure do ask a lot of questions. All I can say is we're paying your old man a visit." He smiled at her. "You'll have to take this as it comes."

Nathan parked the car. Totally confused, she got out. He came around and offered her his arm to escort her into the building. They passed the nurses' station where the men and women she'd seen so many times when visiting her dad grinned looking goofy happy. She and Nathan turned onto the hall to her father's room and Rane stopped. Both sides of the corridor were lined with officers, all standing at attention in their dress uniforms. Denton was there, as was Ben, who gave her a wink as she passed. Bewildered, she let Nathan guide her until she stepped through her father's doorway. Looking around the room, she didn't think she could catch her breath.

Her father stood in his police uniform, the awareness in his eyes telling her he was cognizant of what was going on. Lily stood to the side, beaming widely, a camera in her hand. Next to her father, impossibly tall and broad shouldered in his dress blues, stood Jon.

Nathan released her as she stepped forward. "What's going on?"

Doug Smith looked at Jon, met his gaze, and nodded. Jon reached into his pocket and approached her and went down on one knee. Realization dawned like a thunderclap, and Rane felt her heart stutter and restart with a thud.

Jon cleared his throat, his expression intense. "Rane, sweetheart, light of my life. I love you."

"Jon, oh God, I love you too."

He smiled broadly. "Good, because that makes the rest of this a whole lot easier." He took a breath as if gathering his courage and reached for her hand, speaking in a clear voice. "Rane, would you do me the great honor of marrying me? Will you be my wife, my partner for life, make a family with me, grow old with me?"

Rane felt like she would burst with happiness. Here was the man she loved offering himself and a future she'd only dreamed of. Refusing to allow herself to cry, she took a deep breath and let go of all the what ifs and dove in headfirst.

"Yes, I'll marry you. I love you. I want you. I want a family. I want a future with you." She gripped his hand to pull him to his feet.

He took the ring, an emerald surrounded by small diamonds, and slipped it onto her finger, and then bent his head to kiss her to the claps and whistles of the crowd that had gathered at the door.

Rane wrapped her arms around his neck and he wrapped his around her to swing her off her feet. When he set her down he pulled back to look into her eyes. "Be sure, because there's no going back."

She placed her hands on either side of his face and pressed another kiss to his lips. "I don't want to go back. I want to go forward with you."

He kissed her again and Rane felt her world settle into place.

Jon held her close and she was exactly where she wanted to be.

Epilogue

"What the hell are you doing up there? You're scaring the crap out of me. Will you come off that ladder?"

Rane looked down into flashing blue eyes. "I want to finish this window."

"I'll finish the window. Come down. Now."

"Jon, really. You're overreacting."

"Down, Rane." He paused. "Please."

She heaved a sigh and set the can of sealer on the ladder shelf before carefully starting down. When her feet were once again planted on the ground, she turned to her husband, hands on her hips.

The news she had to tell him was bubbling up in her throat, ready to shoot out of her mouth. She wanted to tell him *right*. Not when he was tired and edgy after a tough shift.

She tried for placating. "You can't wrap me in cotton wool for the next six months, you know. I have good balance and I was being careful." Winter had put her project on hold but now that it was warming up again she was determined that the house would be done before her due date.

"If wrapping you in cotton wool is what it takes, I'll do it. Why don't you go get some of that decaf iced tea I made this morning and you can sit on the porch. I'll finish the window. Besides, you should put your feet up. The doctor said it's good for you to put your feet up, and to go for walks. We'll take Cooper for a walk later when it cools down, before we go visit your dad."

"You'll make yourself a nervous wreck if you obsess during this entire pregnancy, you know."

"In this case obsessing is good. When you're sitting down you can tell me how today's doctor's appointment went since I couldn't make it."

"Okay, okay, you win. I'll be back in a sec." Rane went into the house and returned with two glasses of tea, ice tinkling as she walked. She'd wanted to finish the window, but now that she was out of the sun she could admit the cool shade of the porch felt good. Jon, dressed in jeans torn at the knee and a faded red t-shirt, climbed to the top of the ladder.

He and Nathan had been undercover for the past week and were close to breaking a case. He probably wanted to get a beer and relax, yet here he was putting sealer on the window frame. She wondered if maybe she should wait to tell him until he wasn't under so much stress. Nah. There was no way she could keep such a big secret, and he deserved to know.

She watched the play of muscles in his arms as he plied the brush with easy strokes. "It would go faster with both of us working on it, you know."

He shot her a look and continued to apply the sealer. "If you don't agree to take it easy I'm going to handcuff you to the bedpost."

She thought about that. "I don't suppose you mean handcuffing me to the bedpost in the fun way, do you?"

This time the look he sent her was slightly wicked. Rane drank her iced tea and waved to Mrs. Kershaw and Honey Pumpkin walking down the sidewalk on the far side of the street.

Jon finished the window and put the lid on the sealer before descending the ladder. He climbed the steps to the porch and sat next to her, reaching out to take a glass and draining the tea. He leaned back in the love seat with his arm draped behind her and looked at her with his sexy smile that melted her heart every time.

"How ya doin', sweetheart?"

She smiled as he twirled a lock of her hair around his finger. "Fine and dandy."

"Good, me too." Still smiling, he reached out a hand to cover the swell of her belly, massaging gently.

"We're having twins." The words flew out of her mouth before she had time to ease into the topic. From the look on Jon's face she didn't think he'd have been more stunned if she'd told him she was from another planet.

"What? Twins? That's not possible." He looked down at her belly as if he could somehow see the truth there.

"It certainly is possible, and is actually a certainty." She turned toward him and gripped his hands. "I heard two heartbeats today."

Rane waited. She'd had much the same response when the nurse had said she thought she could hear more than one heartbeat.

Jon's expression was still stunned when he looked back at her. "Twins? Really?"

"Yep, twins"

His grin flashed brilliantly. "We made babies."

"That we did."

"We made two babies. We're getting a two-fer. Two for the price of one. Twice the bang for the buck." He sat for a moment, looking dazed, then abruptly took her face between his hands to deliver a smacking kiss. He pulled back to look her in the eyes, his fingers lingering in her hair. "I don't think I've ever been this happy. I love you. I love our babies. Holy shit. I'm going to be the father of twins."

Rane wrapped her arms around her husband's shoulders and held him close. She thought of all that had happened in the past six months, all the changes in her life, and through it all he had been her center. "I love you," she told him.

The roar of a motorcycle had them pulling apart. Jon groaned. "Here comes my badass brother. The guy goes weak in the knees when he finds out you're pregnant and starts treating you like you'd break if you so much as flexed a muscle. When he hears it's twins he won't let you feed yourself, let alone climb a ladder."

"I never knew the Garretson men were such worriers."

"It's because we love you, sweetheart."

Taking her hand, Jon helped her to her feet as the motorcycle pulled into the driveway. Rane leaned back against Jon, his arms crossed in front of her, his cheek resting against her hair while they waited for Nathan to join them.

Rane had given up wondering how she had gotten so lucky and vowed she'd never take what she had for granted. Her life had taken a wonderful turn and she would embrace it and her new family with everything she could.

She had married an amazing man. His family had welcomed her with open arms, and her dad knew she was happy.

Now with her babies tucked safely in her womb, her world was complete.

TURN THE PAGE FOR A SNEAK PEEK AT

HIDDEN LOYALTY

HIDDEN LOYALTY

Bella was a pro at hiding her emotions, which was absolutely crucial given her current assignment. Her job this weekend? Be the knockout arm candy to the man in the driver's seat next to her. A man who wore sexy and remote as smoothly as James Bond.

Chief Deputy US Marshal Seth Jameson, her boss, her current partner, the man who equally intrigued and infuriated her, had his gaze focused on the road winding ahead of them. Which she knew was misleading. While he *appeared* to be thinking only of mastering the two-tone red and black Bugatti Chiron, she was one hundred percent positive his brain was reviewing and re-reviewing their plan to take into custody the elusive and dangerous fugitive they were tracking.

Their mission was dangerous. Maybe the most dangerous of her career, and she needed to emulate Seth's monumental focus to make sure she acted exactly as she'd been coached.

Tonight's task was to gain access to and arrest the incredibly wealthy, eccentric, and heavily guarded fugitive, Hugo Montenegro. The first step had been achieved. Seth had constructed a fictitious background as a fabulously wealthy antiquities trader, one who didn't mind skirting the boundaries of what was legal to commandeer items particularly desired by his clients.

Montenegro's interest was in instruments of death, especially those used in ceremonial deaths or notorious killings. Seth had learned of Montenegro's obsession with one item and had been able to use that as leverage to obtain an invitation to his home.

Bella's job was to appear decorative. Normally, when working she maintained a professional demeanor, as dictated by the policy directives of her employer. That meant wearing clothing that projected a positive image of the Marshals Service to the public and that didn't draw attention to herself.

For this assignment, however, lowkey and staid had been thrown out the window. She'd prepared carefully, using the stipend allotted to her to purchase attire that would highlight her assets. She had the makeup and accessories to help create the look she'd wear for their overnight stay.

The kickoff was a formal dinner party, and she thought she'd hit the mark for that event. Her hair was pinned at the back of her head in a sophisticated upsweep that showed off her neck. She'd left a few stray curls artfully arranged for interest. She'd used copious amounts of mascara and eye shadow to accentuate the shape and the color of her eyes, making them appear more exotic and a deeper blue, and she'd selected crimson red lipstick to draw attention to her mouth.

Her long dress gleamed an iridescent blue that reminded her of peacock feathers and showcased her curves, emphasizing the narrowness of her waist before flaring up, and with the help of an amazing bra, lifting her breasts like a sacrificial offering.

When she'd opened the door of her hotel room to Seth's knock, there'd been a moment when she thought he'd been caught off guard. For a span of time that'd been mere seconds, his slate gray eyes had flashed, generating a blistering heat as they'd swept her body from head to toe. By the time that gaze had met hers, any reaction to her appearance was walled off.

The ice man had returned.

His appearance had hit her equally as hard. Lust zapped her with a white-hot jolt when she'd opened her door to find him standing tall and impossibly handsome in black tie. The formalwear should have tamed him, made him look refined and polished, but somehow the smooth black jacket and the stiff white cuffs only served to provide a thin veneer of civilization.

Surreptitiously, she studied his profile which seemed to have been carved of the same granite as the home they were nearing. If she was a pro at hiding her emotions, Seth Jameson was a master. Which made her wonder if she was the only one to sense the strong emotions kept locked behind a fortress wall.

She gave an involuntary start when he reached out to grip her hand.

He raised his arched brow. "You're messing with the ring. It looks like you're not used to it. Montenegro will notice that. He'll notice everything about you."

"That's the point, isn't it? He's hypersexual, and we're counting on him noticing me. I can distract him, and he might say things to me he wouldn't say to you."

"Right." He returned his hand to the steering wheel. A muscle worked his jaw. "You nervous?"

"A little, but you'll be there." His gaze flicked over her and she shrugged. "I'll do my job."

"No doubt."

They followed the curve of the driveway to the front of the house. Big men in dark blazers and sunglasses with mirrored lenses stood at strategic spots—an upstairs balcony, the front entrance, and a walkway that rounded the corner of the house. Hugo Montenegro was taking no chances with his safety. He was a high-value fugitive shining a spotlight on himself this evening.

Seth pulled to a stop behind a high-end Benz. A valet elbowed a colleague to the side for the chance to drive the Bugatti. The young man stepped forward but Seth held him off with a raised hand. Instead of reaching for the door handle, he turned to face her. "We'll be sharing a bedroom."

"We've talked about this, sir. I know what to expect."

"Call me Stephen, even if you think we can't be overheard. You never know where there might be listening devices. We're Stephen Braddock and Anna Novak." Dark brows lowered over his stone-gray eyes. "It's more than the bedroom. We have to display a believable level of intimacy. As you said, Montenegro is hypersexual and he'll be aware of a beautiful woman. You're supposed to distract him, but that's as far as it goes. The best way to keep him from attempting anything more is for you to stay close to me and make sure he knows you're mine. The story of our recent engagement will support that."

"I'll play my part, *Stephen*. You play yours. If you can convince him that you have what he wants, we'll be able to complete this assignment and go home."

He glanced out the window. "The valet is watching. We start now." He leaned forward and pressed his mouth to hers. The shock made her rigid, then heat flashed and her lips moved under his. The hair at the back of his head, the deliciously thick hair she'd had secret fantasies about, slid through her fingers.

He broke the kiss and moved back, a look crossing his face that was gone in a heartbeat. If she didn't know better, she'd say it was stark hunger. But, as he'd said, acting their parts was critical, and he'd already started.

She gathered her composure, nonchalantly rubbing her thumb across the skin at the corner of his mouth. "Can't have you going to a dinner party with lipstick smeared on your mouth, darling."

"Right. Let's go."

ABOUT THE AUTHOR

USA TODAY Bestselling Author, Diane Benefiel has been an avid reader all her life. She enjoys a wide range of genres, from westerns to fantasy to mysteries, but romance is her favorite. She writes what she loves best to read—emotional, heart-gripping romantic suspense novels. In her stories, she puts the heroes and heroines in all sorts of predicaments that they have to work together to overcome. Her novel, **Solitary Man** was a National Readers' Choice Award winner.

A native Southern Californian, Diane enjoys nothing better than summer. For a high school history teacher, summer means a break from students, and time immersed in her current writing project. With both kids grown and gone, she enjoys her leisure time camping, especially in the Sierras, and gardening, both with her husband.

Diane loves hearing from her readers.

Website: dianebenefiel.com
Twitter: twitter.com/dianebenefiel
Instagram: diane_benefiel
Pinterest: diane_benefiel
Facebook: facebook.com/DianeBenefielRomance
BookBub: bookbub.com/authors/diane-benefiel
Goodreads: goodreads.com/author/show/8075321.Diane_Benefiel
Newsletter: https://landing.mailerlite.com/webforms/landing/n1i2u8

Boroughs Publishing Group

www.BOROUGHSPUBLISHINGGROUP.com

If you enjoyed this book, please write a review. Our authors appreciate the feedback, and it helps future readers find books they love. We welcome your comments and invite you to send them to info@boroughspublishinggroup.com. Follow us on Facebook, Twitter and Instagram, and be sure to sign up for our newsletter for surprises and new releases from your favorite authors.

Are you an aspiring writer? Check out www.boroughspublishinggroup.com/submit and see if we can help you make your dreams come true.

Made in United States
North Haven, CT
01 April 2025